George Lincoln

WHO NEEDS FLOWERS WHEN THEY'RE DEAD?

Vanguard Press

A CIP catalogue record for this title is
available from the British Library.

ISBN 97 8 1784656 08 9

Vanguard Press is an imprint of
Pegasus Elliot MacKenzie Publishers Ltd.
www.pegasuspublishers.com

First Published in 2019

Vanguard Press
Sheraton House Castle Park
Cambridge England

Printed & Bound in Great Britain

For Atinus

CHAPTER 1

It made no sense whatsoever. A miserable fucking bus depot in the middle of nowhere on a cold, wet winter afternoon. He trudged in there like a naughty boy sent to see the headmaster, full of fear and trepidation.

'No, I am not lost,' he said in response to the rather bemused-looking receptionist's polite enquiry.

He hated the way adults always patronised him, as if all he needed to succeed in life was a fucking compass.

'We don't get many boys in here your age, you know,' said the receptionist.

By now the naive confusion of a pale, skinny fourteen-year-old was growing by the second into the full-blown humiliation of not really understanding why the fuck he was standing there in the first place.

'I came to collect something for my dad.' He just-about managed to stutter the line repeatedly drilled into his ear for the past half an hour in the car on the way there.

'Oh really? Most of our drivers come here to collect their own belongings, you know.'

Of course they fucking do. As if he needed to be told this. But this perfectly reasonable, predictable line of enquiry would never enter his dad's head, mostly because it got in the way of what he wanted at that particular time. Which is all that ever mattered.

'I came to collect his pay.' The words somehow eventually tumbled out of the boy's mouth. 'His severance pay,' he managed to add, almost forgetting his line.

'And your dad couldn't come to collect this himself, no?'

'No, he is very unwell today.'

The boy remembered his line this time.

Ten minutes later the boy was sitting in the car as his dad ripped open the brown envelope as though it contained the winning lottery ticket. For a brief moment the boy glowed in the warm feeling that he had done something that made his dad happy. But this feeling was short-lived as his dad glared with what seemed like genuine astonishment at a cheque for just £8.72. Of course this was the boy's fault. He hadn't explained things properly to the kind lady at reception. He should probably go back inside and ask if the one thousand five hundred pounds deduction from final pay for bus driver training in lieu was a mistake. Far better if this came from the boy than from the spineless fucking coward waiting in the car park who quit the job after just three months.

Rage infused every fibre of his father's being at this apparent injustice, the way the boy had seen so many times before. By now the boy wasn't listening any more, just gazing up towards the window of the office he'd been in a few moments ago. He noticed how a line of people had gathered to see the envelope-opening ceremony in full for themselves.

He'd heard all of this before.

There wouldn't be enough money for him to have anything nice this month. It wasn't because his dad hadn't quite negotiated the basic requirements of his new job properly by driving a big yellow bus around the Peak District without getting lost like a fucking moron. It wasn't because his dad didn't feel he needed to attend extra training sessions and perhaps spend more time learning his bus routes.

It was because he had a son who hadn't quite developed into the accomplished liar his dad was just yet.

CHAPTER 2

David was fascinated by what drove people to commit the most sordid, evil crimes and by some amazing good fortune he had the perfect job to indulge his interest – a detective in the Metropolitan Police Service. The boys in blue. The thin blue line. Or the fucking filth, depending on your own perspective.

David can't remember which way round events unfolded, so much of his childhood a blurred memory. Did he seek out the specific role that would grant him unlimited access to these crime scenes, the unadulterated sorrow of the family members left behind by the tragedy in question? Or was there something dark that he found himself subconsciously drawn towards, long before he began to realise he *enjoyed* it? Such questions for a future inquest perhaps. All David knew for sure was that he loved his job but it was for all the wrong reasons. Trapped in a paradigm of false expectations and secret desires, trying to 'fit in' as much as he possibly could without ever raising too much alarm. It was tricky.

It's not that David wanted anybody to suffer, least of all complete strangers he had never met. But once he realised that suffering was such an integral part of the human condition, David began to view the suffering of others as some warped idea of free *entertainment*. He didn't create or wish for the suffering to occur, he merely extracted what he needed for his own gratification at no cost to any other being, living or not so.

This was how it began.

Politicians and senior police officers came and went, each promising to be tough on crime, to stamp out crime, to eradicate all human error, to shape all human thought along a more 'acceptable' trajectory for future generations. And the general public would buy into this constant war footing, this notion that in order to survive and protect what we have, there must be some 'other' to all rally against.

It's not that David disagreed with any of this. He just felt that the general public were missing out on the essence of what human suffering has to offer. Only through experiencing directly the true suffering of others can we possibly hope to value what is ours and by definition, the suffering that we do *not* have to endure ourselves.

But none of this made David a popular choice at social events and team-building exercises. When faced with the darkness or the everlasting light, most people don't like having to use their torch if they don't have to. David wanted to shine a light on all things, no matter how well the darkness hid them. In his uniform patrol

13

days, after seeing the aftermath of a horrific car accident with untold misery and devastation splattered all over the windscreen, David would volunteer to seek out the family members just so he could deliver the news and bask in the immediate abject crushing misery that unfolded for free in front of his very own eyes. He wanted to dwell as deeply as possible in the misery and devastation. It's not a job people usually volunteer for and even the most sadistic supervising officer would be loath to order somebody to do this. Which is not to say David felt they were wrong to feel this way, he just felt it was a shame they were missing out on all the best bits.

David got used to being side-lined in the workplace due to his 'interests'. But he worked this to his advantage, allowing him more time to delve deep into the rabbit hole of human suffering unhindered by the emotional boundaries other people seemed to possess. When colleagues tried to use jokes and banter to make light of something horrific, David felt sad for them. Sad for their inability to breathe in the misery, to be a sponge of desolation and despair the way he was.

Rape. Incest. Sexual slavery. Torture. Human trafficking. Child abuse. These were the big-hitters, the heavyweights. People get over losing a bar fight or crashing their car or having their handbag stolen. They never forget the humiliation of being raped. The suffering of being forced to submit to something so degrading stays with the victim forever.

Having worked his way through the organisation, by 2012 David was a detective in the Sexual Offences & Child Abuse Investigation Command. An Olympic year. Every single day a goldmine of untapped misery just waiting to be laid bare. Thanks to the post-2008 financial meltdown and the swingeing cuts to police budgets that soon followed, they couldn't wait to deliver David with a smorgasbord of suffering from the day he arrived. Historic rape of a child by a teacher? Yes, please. Anal rape of a broken woman by her uncle? Lovely. Suicide by ramming a CD case so far up her own cunt that she bled out in the mental hospital where staff had been raping her for years? Manna from heaven.

And this is where it really began for David. Everything in his life leading up to that point had been preparation for the tidal wave of sorrow that was about to wash over him.

CHAPTER 3

'I'd rather have a dead son than one who is fucking queer.'

His dad's words hit him like a bullet to the brain. The boy had recently discovered bands like The Cure and Black Sabbath, bands not known for the traditional notion that only women wore make-up. He immersed himself in the whole new world these and many other bands had to offer boys his age in the early 1990s. Boys in make-up seemed so other-worldly, so out-there to him. There was even a special episode on Trisha one day.

Of course, in his dad's eyes, this made him a homosexual. He had grown up surrounded by photos of relatives standing proudly outside the many steelworks and coal mines once so abundant in the area. It seemed like they all had dark circles around their eyes and black fingernails. He'd just be carrying on the family tradition, he thought. His dad did not see it that way.

His dad was more into 'proper' music like David Bowie.

The boy was the older of two brothers born three years apart. Both had taken their parents' divorce hard, shattering any sense of stability and normality they had clung to even through the years of endless tension. The boys were no strangers to anger, having grown up around it for most of their lives. The younger of the two boys had taken the break-up particularly badly and tried to find solace in recreational drugs. Speed. Ecstasy. Amphetamines. He even sniffed glue when all else failed. Several visits to the hospital to collect what was left of their younger son from the emergency room didn't bring his parents any closer together.

The boy didn't wear his make-up at home again.

CHAPTER 4

Sally had been in and out of various psychiatric institutions for most of her tragically short teenage years. Born to heroin-addicted parents, her time with them had been thankfully brief before social services intervened. The depths of self-delusion that crack addicts often possess never ceased to amaze David. He was in no position to condemn others for an unhealthy addiction. He understood that all too well. But his addiction bore no consequence for the lives of others, unlike a baby born addicted to smack.

Sally had shown early signs of promise, spending most of her pre-teenage years with one long-term adoptive carer, Susan. The thing they don't really prepare you for as an adoptive parent is the resentment and anger your child will always feel towards the world and, by extension, towards you. You weren't there in the beginning. You aren't my real mum. The second that child reaches puberty and all those hormones come flooding forward, you're at the top of the shit-list.

Which is exactly the position Susan found herself in.

Sally had always been very creative in both art and literature, showing great potential as a writer. She wrote pages and pages of rather graphic stories about a girl her age repeatedly raped and abused. Always in the third person.

People began to notice.

Sally slowly ostracised herself from any recognisable peer group, consumed by her writing. Teachers would enquire, refer and forget. Social workers went through the same process. Nobody seemed able to get through to Sally; she was lost in her stories.

With no visible signs of injury or abuse, bureaucratic hands were tied. Susan watched her adopted daughter disappear into substance abuse. Sally stopped going to school, preferring instead to write. She now began to add drawings and sketches to her stories. Little teenage doodles of a young girl tied to a ceiling light, clothes ripped open. Vaginal tears. Location unknown.

Substance abuse inevitably led to psychiatric referral when Sally became violent. Institutionalised by the age of fourteen. Then the line between what was real and what she imagined became forever blurred for Sally.

David read the file with such fervour he quickly forgot about any other cases he had. This was the one. Sally's stories, complete with drawings, had been lovingly bound as one long book of police exhibit misery. Exhibits were supposed to be stored securely at all times, with a clear chain of evidence linking any removal from storage for any reason. Without this there could never be any trial, too easy for a defence barrister to pull the case apart. David pored over each and every word, absorbing each little pocket of despair. Ostensibly, he was taking the case very seriously. Nobody could ever accuse him of not being thorough. He needed to get closer. He needed to soak up every last drop of Sally that he could.

'Thank you so much for allowing me into your home.'

David politely wiped his feet at the door. The small meaningless gestures we make, he wondered to himself. Not much mud in this part of London.

'Have you travelled far?'

The meaningless patter continued, Susan knowing exactly where he had travelled from. People seem to find comfort in such predictable words and gestures. Like leaving flowers on a grave long after that person has died. Who are those flowers really for?

Sally's bedroom had been left the way she always preferred it. The air was stale as if the windows had been closed for quite some time. Susan said she could never bring herself to change anything, even after Sally left. Apparently, this included the air in the room. Air with sentimental value. Immaculately presented in white, as an estate agent might say.

No posters, David noticed. As though Sally didn't want any other pairs of eyes to see her, living or otherwise.

Intensely private, like a womb of teenage dreams. His eyes darted around the room for any nuance that might unlock some darker secret. There was nothing.

Small cracks beginning to appear in the coving. The tell-tale signs of wall filler over an old picture hanger opposite the window. The slightly dated feel suggested a teenager raised by somebody significantly older, from a different generation. You could imagine those creepy old Victorian dolls, lace doilies and net curtains if Sally had never lived there. Sally saving Susan from her own taste.

He sat on the crisp white bed linen. An array of cute teddy bears along the fold below the pillow. He breathed in deeply, the faint aroma of sickly-sweet teenage perfume seemed to have been released into the air by him sitting on the bed. He was probably the first person to do so for a long time. Susan tried to busy herself, tidying what was already tidy, shuffling around uncomfortably. David was reminded how normal parents often behaved around strangers, terrified of any negative judgement being directed towards them.

Just days earlier, Sally lay in pools of her own blood, undiscovered for several hours at the secure unit she had been detained at. The latest Jewel CD rammed so far inside her uterus the medical team later said they wouldn't have been able to retrieve it if she had survived, the blood loss would have been so heavy.

'Can I offer you anything to drink, Officer?'

Another polite gesture.

'I'm okay, thank you,' David replied, mildly irritated at the interruption to his thoughts.

Though not technically part of any crime scene, he had hoped the bedroom would offer him more of Sally. It seemed she had taken anything really personal with her, leaving just the pretty picture she wanted the world to think of her behind.

'Sally would never have committed suicide,' Susan tentatively suggested.

'Why do you think this?'

David humoured her. A locked room in a secure psychiatric unit with twenty-four-hour CCTV coverage showing all access to her room. Showing her entering her room shortly before midnight. Showing no hourly checks whatsoever until her body was discovered by the morning team shortly after six a.m. Sally was supposed to be checked hourly due to her being deemed a high suicide risk following the death of her friend a few weeks earlier. They had been standing on the platform at Denmark Hill station together, a suicide pact about to unfold in front of a thousand commuters. Her friend jumped first.

Sally hesitated.

She would later tell her grief counsellor that she didn't think her friend was being serious. She blamed herself for her friend's death, as teenage girls so often do. Then she went on to make allegations of repeated sexual abuse at the hands of every male staff member and even her own brother, a serving police officer. All in rooms covered by CCTV at all times, which was the reason David was at Sally's house that day.

'She was always so happy to be alive, so full of life,' Susan replied with the love and certainty only a mother could.

David was not a monster. He vaguely recalled what a loving mother might think, what they might choose to believe and what they would want to cling on to for years afterwards as some sort of coping mechanism. They say the truth hurts and so often it really does. Susan was just trying to get through each day.

'Did you find what you were looking for, Officer?' Susan enquired as David stood and walked towards the door.

'Thank you for allowing me into what must be such a sacred space for you,' he deflected.

He couldn't discuss details of the case at this stage, and she knew that. He had noticed the Christian adornments on the walls downstairs and thought she might appreciate the use of the word 'sacred'. Total victim care to the end.

As he drove back to the station, a feeling of dissatisfaction seemed to linger. Sally had been given every opportunity to succeed in life. She had an adoptive mother who loved her very much, despite the crack-addicted womb from where she had first emerged into the world. She showed promise at school and had a lovely home life with white walls and white bed linen. She was loved so much even the fucking air in her bedroom had sentimental value. How dare she throw all of this away. Suicide was for losers, weaklings who gave up. Although a small part of him admired the intensely grotesque way she chose to end it. That took balls.

He returned her book to the evidence room. He'd crossed the t's and dotted the i's. There were no witnesses to any of the stories Sally wrote. Her grotesque suicide set a precedent at Kings College Hospital for any other woman in the future who decided she needed a new place to store her CD collection. He'd visited the scene. A far cry from the loving home Susan had provided her with. The cold, hard feel of an institutional bedroom. Grilled windows. Polished steel mirrors. CCTV may have shown a lackadaisical approach to patient care but no suggestion any third party was involved in her death, or indeed any other story she wrote.

But that death was something.

David read the medical report over and over again. The severity of stabbing depends on the point of entry, which organ has been injured, shape and sharpness of the penetrating object and finally is the penetrating object still in the wound or has it been taken out? In most cases, if the stabbing object penetrates through the chest wall, hurting intercostal blood vessels, you can expect to see pneumothorax or hemopneumothorax.

David no longer felt like an interloper, prying into people's deeply disturbing and tragic moments.

These were now his moments.

CHAPTER 5

Lloyd seemed like he had done this before as he led the way through some undergrowth, towards a large brown building with no windows. Nobody would see them behind here. The boy remembered wondering why only he had been asked along that day when all his other friends were off school for the summer as well. They all wanted a go on that bike as much as he did. Lloyd was one of the older boys on the estate. The boy knew nobody would mess with him when he was with Lloyd because he was bigger than everybody else and didn't even have to worry about getting kicked out of school any more since he had left for good that summer.

The boy felt safe around Lloyd.

All the local kids knew this as the 'waterworks', an old water treatment centre at the end of the street the boy lived in. Years later they put great big steel railings all around it because of the constant graffiti and property damage. Boys will be boys.

They reached a small verge and Lloyd stopped walking, turning to the boy and gesturing for him to stop. The boy looked around for something, anything.

Just grass and plenty of high bushes between them and anything else.

'Do you know what big boys do?'

The boy didn't really understand the question Lloyd had just asked him. All he cared about was having a go on Lloyd's silver Mongoose BMX. It was brand new, and Lloyd had said he could have a go on it if he did something for him first. All the other kids would be so jealous. His mum had promised him a new bike for his birthday which was coming up soon but that seemed like ages away. And he knew they couldn't afford a Mongoose so it would probably be something rubbish anyway.

'I'm going to show you something. If you run away or shout, I'll kick your little fucking head in.'

The boy nodded his acceptance of these terms. He remembered whenever they played football here at the waterworks, his mum always used to tell him off for wandering over towards the buildings. He never really understood why. Lloyd began to undo his belt and unzipped his flies. He pulled out what seemed like the biggest cock the boy had ever seen.

'I want you to hold this for me,' said Lloyd, his tone a little gentler this time.

The boy really didn't understand how this had anything to do with the bike. Lloyd began stroking this giant fucking cock gently up and down with his hand, staring at the boy intensely as he did so. The boy felt awkward. Lloyd was his friend. He always used to come hang around with the younger kids when they were playing on the swings or playing football. He always seemed quite calm and friendly but this felt different. The boy wasn't sure what was happening.

'Are you going to hold it or not?'

'Not if you're going to piss on me, no,' was the boy's main concern.

There was this boy at school who pissed all over himself a few days ago. There was no way the boy was going to let that happen to him. His mum would've killed him.

'I promise I won't piss on you,' the older boy laughed, still stroking his giant cock gently up and down. The boy had seen cocks like this in some magazines they found behind the shops a few weeks ago. All these naked women lying there with their tits and fannies out, some guy with a massive cock dangling in their face. His mum was really angry with him when they got caught going through the newsagent's bins; he'd been grounded for a few days.

By now Lloyd had sat down on the grass verge, lying on his back. He was still stroking that massive cock and looking straight at the boy.

'All you have to do is hold it for a bit, that's all.'

The boy felt a bit more at ease now that Lloyd was sitting on the floor. If he did decide to kick his head in, at least the boy had time to run while he fastened his trousers back up.

'That's it?'

'Promise. Then you can have a go on my Mongoose.'

The boy sensed something wasn't quite right but didn't see how this could do him any harm. His mum was always telling him not to wander off with strange men but Lloyd wasn't a stranger; he was his mate. Slowly he reached over and put his hand around Lloyd's cock. It felt really hard. Bigger than anything he had felt in his hand before. Lloyd told him to hold it tighter, so he did. Lloyd seemed to like this a lot and lay back on the grass. He told the boy to start moving his hand up and down, slowly.

The boy's house was really close to here. He usually played out most of the daytime during the school holidays because it was boring just sitting at home. There was this other boy who lived a few doors down from their house called Shaun. Shaun's dad was really loud and would just stand at the front door shouting as loud as he could until Shaun eventually came running home. Sometimes this would go on for half an hour or so. His mum said he was a nice man but didn't realise how loud he was. The boy didn't really like going in their house because it always felt really cramped. They all shared a bedroom with each other, brothers and sisters together. It was a bit weird. Years later Shaun got arrested for having sex with his younger sister.

'Faster, do it faster,' Lloyd said.

Eventually it stopped. The boy couldn't really remember how or why. Just like he said he would, Lloyd let the boy ride around on his Mongoose for a bit. He rode it up to the park where Shaun and his other friends were and gave them all two fingers as he rode past. He brought it back and handed it to Lloyd, who was sitting waiting outside the boy's house.

'If you ever tell anybody about this, I'll kill you.'

CHAPTER 6

Total victim care. This was the Met's commitment to giving each and every victim of crime the proper care they deserved. Regular updates. Professional handling of their case. The legal process explained to them in plain English. Support when needed in attending court. Video evidence played to a jury to prevent the victim having to face his or her attacker in court. Financial support to cover travelling expenses and any loss of earnings when victims were needed in court. Rehearsals, familiarisation visits, requests for wigs and gowns to be removed. Compensation for any injuries sustained, physical or otherwise. Total victim care.

David soon realised his role was far more consuming than anything he had previously been involved in. Sure, 7/7 was a bad day for London. He'd spent twenty-four hours on duty that terrible day, helping to recover what remained of the Aldgate tube bomb victims. The smell of cooked human flesh is not something you ever forget. Unidentifiable pieces of a person's dreams and ambitions scattered all over the twisted iron tracks.

This type of experience tends to focus the mind on the job in hand.

But then you carry on. It's what you get paid for. Abuse victims were something altogether different to David. Everything is hidden. The grooming, planning and preparation involved all goes on in secret. The degrading acts always take place behind closed doors. The years of silence. The threats, the fear, the stigma. Everything so wrapped up in mystery, sometimes forever. What doesn't kill you leaves a big fucking scar across your psyche. You can spend years in therapy and still go home and cry yourself to sleep every day. But only if you choose to be a victim.

David hated the victim culture. Nobody accepts any responsibility any more. Everybody lining up to pour their heart and soul out so they can spend the rest of their lives believing that nothing is their fault. Jimmy fucking Saville. Thousands of people all of a sudden feel compelled to become a victim the second that fucker dropped dead.

Really? The man in the shell suit with a cigar and silver comb-over wasn't quite entirely honourable?

That must have come as a huge shock to so many. But not while he was alive. That would involve courage. That would require facing head-on the person who supposedly ruined your life. Best to wait until they're all dead and then play the victim card with impunity. David wasn't a victim of anything. He despised the weakness and indignity of it all. We all fuck up. Accept this and pick yourself up. Make different choices. Don't pass that choice onto someone else, some 'other' that you can then blame for the rest of your pathetic existence.

Choose not to be a victim like Clare. A fat fuck if David ever saw one. He tried to work out the point at which the red blood vessels in her face would've last been beneath the surface of her dry, broken skin. A face so ravaged by internal suffering and anxiety it had forgotten which parts were supposed to smile and which parts were supposed to cry. Clare was begging for a terminal illness to end her misery. And if she wasn't, she fucking well should be.

Clare had grown up in Ulster, near the Falls Road which is a predominantly Catholic area. Clare had been encouraged by her uncle to meet him in an alleyway numerous times between the ages of eight and thirteen, whereby he had violated her orally, anally and vaginally many times. The abuse only stopped when she moved away with her family to England. Clare never reported it to anybody and instead just slowly disintegrated into what now sat before David in the victim interview suite forty years later.

Clare was a fucking shipwreck, lost at sea with no hope of survival. Alcoholism had ravaged her skin and mental capacity; poor diet had taken her teeth and what may have once been a waistline. Years of chronic depression had taken whatever else had once existed of Clare's personality. Clare could barely speak a sentence without breaking down into floods of tears, which made taking her statement a rather arduous process, not helped by her thick Ulster accent which David hadn't had time to fully acclimatize to yet. How the fuck can 'hand', 'hair' and 'wear' sound the same?

'So why did you never report this matter before, Clare?'

'I'm a Catholic,' came the pitiful response.

David forgot he was relatively lucky. As a white male he'd always enjoyed the privilege of police support growing up in England. Things weren't so simple over the water for Catholics at the height of the Troubles. Nobody ever thinks about the consequences that has for an entire generation of victims whose cries went unheard because they came from the wrong side of the divide. They could definitely teach the English a thing or two about internalising things, thought David.

The uncle was now dead. Clare only came forward after she heard he'd died recently through a family member. Clare thought that with all the publicity surrounding the Jimmy Saville enquiry, now would be a good time to report what happened to her.

'We will make some enquiries and be in touch.'

David thought a lot about this case, especially about the debris that had sat before him in the form of Clare for the past few hours. You see, the problem for most rapists and abusers – hefty prison sentences aside – is they never actually get to see the long-term effects of the fruits of their labour. A child who is sexually abused probably keeps their mouth shut about it, at least for a while. Then the discontent grows inside them and manifests itself in various ways later in life – drug abuse, alcoholism, emotional disengagement, social awkwardness, unhealthy sexual relationships and so on. The abuser rarely sees this, unless your name happens to be Josef Fritzl. The more David thought about this he began to develop a very obvious theory. At least he thought it was obvious. An abuser rarely sees the fruits of their labour. A trusted professional gets to see the entire mess played out on DVD with a freeze frame function. The sorrow. The emptiness. The confusion. The feelings of self-worthlessness.

Total victim care.

CHAPTER 7

'I need to tell you something, Mum.'

The boy didn't really know what he wanted to say, but since the other day with Lloyd he felt like something wasn't right. Something wasn't normal. He knew his dad hated gays and would probably be really angry with him as usual, so he figured he'd tell Mum about it first and then go out with his friends. There was a roller disco on at school tonight.

'Not now. You and your brother need to sit down. Your dad and I have got something to tell you.'

It never seemed like a good time lately. All they ever did was scream and shout at each other, and then his mum would always be crying when the boy went to bed at night. Sometimes they would carry on screaming and shouting at each other, and then the next day his mum would wear her big sunglasses. Those really big silly ones like Mickey Mouse ears, the boy always used to say to her.

But she didn't laugh.

He hoped they were going to split up. Loads of people at school had parents who were divorced; it wasn't a big deal. They got to see their dads at weekends, and their dads always seemed really pleased to see them. He wondered if they would have to move house. He didn't really mind if they did; he didn't really like playing out at the waterworks any more.

He didn't know where his dad was. His mum and dad never seemed to be in the same room any more, unless they were arguing. It was always worse if Wednesday had lost. His dad was a massive SWFC fan, and how well they played each weekend seemed to dictate his mood for the following week. Sometimes his dad would take him to watch Wednesday play, but he didn't really like it much. Everybody there always seemed really angry.

Somebody knocked at the door. It was the boy's friends from school, Scott and Richard. He forgot they were coming around. The boy thought it was funny how boys his age were always so polite when they knock on the door – he'd never heard Scott speak so politely in his life! They wanted to know if the boy was coming to the roller disco with them.

Everybody was going to be there.

The boy looked hopefully towards his mum, who just closed the door on the two boys waiting outside without even saying anything. She used to do that a lot whenever his friends came around to call for him. It was so embarrassing. She always seemed too preoccupied to be nice to people. A lot of his friends refused to come

37

around for him any more; they said their mums had told them not to. The boy always had to go around to their houses instead.

'Just wait at the end of the street. I'll meet you in ten minutes,' the boy managed to say out of the window as his friends walked away.

They nodded their agreement.

Eventually his dad appeared from somewhere, and both he and his mum were sitting on the sofa. They never sat on the sofa together. His dad usually sat in his armchair next to where all the cassettes were and got really annoyed if anyone else sat there. His dad said that the boy could sit in his armchair if he wanted. It must be important, the boy thought to himself.

His younger brother was there too. All three of them sat in a row on the sofa which the boy thought was really weird and seemed unnatural. They had just got new cream leather sofas and the smell of cheap leather still filled the living room. The dog wasn't allowed up on the new sofas, his mum said. The boy just stayed by the window, watching his friends walking away. The boy noticed his dad had his arm around his brother and looked like he had been crying. His dad never cried, except when Wednesday got relegated. He cried loads that day, the boy remembered.

Everybody seemed really tense. Then the boy started worrying that somebody else had told his parents about Lloyd and he was going to be in loads of trouble, and maybe his dad was crying because he hated gays so much and didn't want people to think he had a gay son. The boy wondered if it was that snitch Shaun who lived down the street with the really loud dad. He was always creeping around in bushes and snitching on people. They were a bit strange in that house.

'Your dad and I are not going to live together any more,' his mum eventually said.

She immediately started crying. Then his dad started crying. Then his brother started bawling his head off like a big baby. Nobody was saying anything. They were just all crying. His brother looked like a Stretch Armstrong on the sofa in the middle of his mum and dad who were both trying to pull him over to their side so they could hug him to make him stop crying.

Nobody wanted to hug the boy, who just carried on looking out of the window. He wasn't crying.

'Can I go to the roller disco now?'

CHAPTER 8

When David first joined the Met Police, he had the same noble ambitions to change the world and help people that most other people write on their application forms. The MacPherson Report had taken its toll on police recruitment in the late 1990s, so by the time David decided to join up they were taking pretty much anybody. By some fluke of having been to university, he found himself stomping around a parade square in north London within about three months of having first tentatively sent off his application. They didn't get many graduates joining the police, and he could see why. He fucking hated doing drill. It was a complete waste of time. He never understood why it was so important for everybody to walk and think and act in exactly the same way.

One of the consequences of being so enraptured by the suffering of others is it tends to create distance with others, David later realised. Create Distance. Use Cover. Transmit. That's what the Met Police had taught him about how to deal with knives and weapons. Create Distance. Use Cover. Transmit. Or CUT for the simpletons.

The Met loved a fucking mnemonic, loved to dumb-down and simplify even the simplest thing. As if when faced with the existential threat of a knife-wielding lunatic, David might feel inclined to get closer were it not for his first-class training. Create Distance. Use Cover. Transmit.

David knew how to create distance.

David picked up a few things along the way. People are stupid being the main thing. Stupid people doing stupid things making bad decisions and suffering terrible consequences and seeming genuinely shocked by the outcome. David never really understood how people got so emotionally attached to things or other people. It was usually this attachment that led to the anger, jealousy, rage, or whatever other uncontrollable emotion that stemmed from the attachment in the first place. David liked to think of himself like a ship without an anchor, just floating along and through whatever came in his path. Untethered. He didn't really see the point of being attached to anything, least of all people.

Because eventually everyone either dies or lets you down.

Something David hadn't encountered before he joined the Met was the sheer capacity for vindictive behaviour so many people possessed. Especially women. Men tend to do stupid things like fight, overpower or rape people physically weaker than they are. But women are very different. Lacking the physicality, they go for the complete mind-fuck when somebody really pisses them off. Like Amy. Young girl in her early twenties. Worked her way into the armed protection department, carrying around enough guns and ammo to start a small war every day. Starts shagging her supervising officer, inevitably. It was only a matter of time in such a male stronghold of a department that they would eventually all come sniffing around the young bit of skirt. Rank has its privileges.

One thing the Met loves is order and numbering. Every officer has a number. Every gun has a number. Match the correct gun to the matching officer. Simple. Eventually the Police Sergeant number 9 gets bored of Amy and decides he'd better turn his attention back to the wife and kids. Maybe she wasn't as good in bed as he'd hoped. Maybe he realised she's just a person with problems and worries and unfulfilled ambitions too. Amy takes it hard. Amy takes out Glock number 9 from the armoury and blows the back of her own fucking head off.

It's a tragedy that nobody saw coming. Even with her brains and skull fragments sprayed all over the armoury wall, she's forever made sure that Police Sergeant number 9 won't forget about her.

'A thorough investigation will be carried out and lessons will be learned,' was the standard Met response to these types of incident. David was struck by Amy's commitment. He felt no real sympathy for her – she was an adult who entered knowingly into a situation she should have known would end in tears. In David's mind, she did the honourable thing. Was this a normal way to think, he wondered to himself? Why couldn't he feel sympathy or compassion for her like everybody else?

David met more than a few women not afraid to plunge the depths of humanity to get their own way. Like Colette, who decided one day she'd had enough of her long-term partner, Darrell. They never married of course; she was always hedging her bets something better would come along. Darrell hadn't done anything wrong in particular; she just felt she could do better. There's got to be something better out there for a woman in her forties with no career and two kids living on welfare in this part of London, she reasoned.

Darrell went to stay with his mum, who loved having the grandchildren over every Sunday so she could cook their favourite dinner. Grandma loved to cook. This went on for a few weeks until Colette grew frustrated with the local authority's decision not to re-house her in a nicer area, especially as Darrell had made a convincing claim that he could provide a more stable home for them with him and their grandma together. A child custody case beckoned. Colette thought she noticed a bruise on the younger child's ankle that wasn't there before they left to see their dad. The only logical conclusion must be that he was beating his own children and trying to hide it under their trouser legs, safe in the knowledge that their mother would never think to look there. No history of reported abuse. The court must be made aware of this, she thought. He had the stable home environment and career to provide for the children, so why wouldn't he start beating them now on their weekend visits?

Colette contacted the police and eventually the case lands on David's desk. David knows how mothers can fail their children without ever intending to. Medical reports are gathered and statements taken from the children concerned. They have been coached. Nothing suspicious here. Even the child doesn't know how the small bruise on her ankle got there. Colette is incandescent.

'Can't you see? They are much safer living with me.'

Case. Fucking. Closed. No suffering for David to revel in here. He has learnt to see it on the victims' faces and knows when it's real by now. Hour after hour playing and re-playing Clare's video statement taught him that much. Absorbed in every last detail, the minutia of anguish writ large across the poor victim's face. Colette's twisted malevolent intentions all too obvious to David, using their young children as pawns to hurt Darrell in the worst way. They tell you to have faith in the legal system and that everybody gets what's fair in the end. David disagreed. Colette never got taken out and gang-raped by Darrell's buddies. David thinks that would have been a fair outcome. And maybe she gets to visit them at Grandma's house at the weekend, under supervision.

But no family court judge will ever pass the sentence that's fair.

Darrell only sees his children at weekends now. They still love Grandma's cooking. Darrell a shadow of his former self. Unable and afraid to trust anybody, unwilling to allow anybody to get too close for fear that they would twist the knife in his back even deeper. Lies awake at night re-playing over and over in his head the day he was arrested on suspicion of abusing his own beloved children. It wasn't the officer's fault; he was just doing his job, following procedure, trying to protect the children.

Create Distance. Use Cover. Transmit.

CHAPTER 9

The boy arrived home from school to find his clothes in two black bin-bags on the doorstep of his house. The boy's entire existence lovingly dumped at the front door by his mother earlier that afternoon. She didn't even bother to put his Narnia books in there. There was a taxi already waiting for him, engine idling impatiently.

'Now you go and live with your dad,' his mum said.

Deep down this was what he wanted, although not quite like this. Since his dad left two years ago, the boy's relationship with his mother had deteriorated rapidly. He blamed her for his dad leaving. She was always arguing and making everything so difficult, he told her. No wonder Dad left, he would say. His dad would never have hit her. She was making it all up for attention, the boy said to her. At least that's what his dad had told him, and why would he lie? The fourteen-year-old boy had the choice of believing he had a violent, abusive father or a delusional mother. Or both.

The boy had arrived home from school that day the same as any other, wondering why everyone in his class was so stupid compared to him. Ever since his friend

Alan left to go to a private school, the boy was easily top of his class in everything. Alan's dad was a doctor and his mum a university professor so the boy didn't really mind being second-place to their son at school. He accepted this as the natural order of things. They had this massive house that he used to go over and play in sometimes; it was like a mansion compared to any other house he'd ever been inside. He always felt a bit embarrassed when Alan came over to play at his house because Alan always used to make fun of how small it was.

He was thinking he would probably go to his other friend, Jonathan's, after tea that day. Jonathan had just got the new Amiga 500, and his mum used to let everyone come around and play on it. Jonathan's mum was really nice but she got really angry once when they all drank from her liquor cabinet one evening. But she got over it and didn't mind Jonathan's friends all coming around, although the liquor cabinet had a lock on it now. The boy's mum never let any of his friends come to his house any more.

Home was just a five-minute walk from school. He never understood people who travelled miles and miles by car or bus to school every day. His favourite subject was maths, mainly because his maths teacher had huge tits, so he would often stay behind after school for extra tuition with her. He was pretty sure that she knew he fancied her, but she didn't seem to mind. One day he wrote 'Miss you have got amazing tits' in the back of his maths book, and when he checked a few days later she had written in red pen 'thanks'. Sometimes she would get these really bad migraines and just lie on her desk for the whole lesson. The boy would spend most of those lessons just gazing at her huge tits and the way her dress would seem to barely contain them, like someone had laid a small hanky over a pair of those massive oranges his mum used to buy sometimes. He'd never had a teacher he fancied before and besides, it was better than going home.

The taxi ride seemed to take ages. He didn't cry though, just thought about what his dad would make him for tea. His dad was always saying how much better it would be if the boy came to live with him because then the council would give him a bigger house, and he'd get more money to buy nicer things if the boy was living with him permanently. The boy didn't understand why his mum didn't just let him go and live with his dad when he first left two years ago if she was just going to throw him out anyway. He didn't really care any more; he was glad. He wouldn't have to live with his stupid brother, and his dad was always saying they would do loads of fun things when he came to live there. Eventually they arrived at his dad's flat on the other side of town. It was miles away from school and only had one bedroom so he would have to sleep on the sofa until they got given a bigger place, which shouldn't take very long, his dad said.

At first things were great. The boy got used to walking a lot further to school but he didn't really mind. His dad didn't really understand how to cook a meal for just two people, so they always ended up eating massive portions. The boy said maybe it was too much, but his dad would get angry if any food got wasted so he just ate it. He didn't really like sleeping on the sofa; he missed having his own room. He wasn't allowed to put any posters up or anything, so he just had to put up with his dad's pictures of pigs and dogs playing snooker. His dad had a thing about pigs which the boy always thought was a bit strange. He'd never been in anybody else's house that had pictures of pigs all over the place. His dad said the boy should be grateful he agreed to look after him and stop complaining. The boy didn't really understand this. His dad used to always say he *wanted* the boy to come and live with him.

His dad started seeing some woman called Karin. She lived miles away and had three kids of her own, so there wasn't much space for the boy to go and visit, his dad said. His dad started spending most evenings staying with her after a while. At first it was just Wednesdays and Saturdays. Then it was Fridays. Then Mondays. And then most Tuesdays. Eventually his dad barely ever stayed at home any more, unless one of Karin's kids had done something to annoy him.

The boy spent most of his time alone.

He was too far away from most of his friends' houses since he moved to be with his dad, and the buses were rubbish. At least he got to sleep in his dad's empty bed most of the time which was much more comfortable than the sofa, and he didn't have to eat so much. As time went on, he ate less and less. How much food he chose to eat was something he could control, he thought to himself. The kind dinner ladies at school always used to try and encourage him to use up his full free school meals allowance, but the boy just didn't feel that hungry.

The boy didn't speak to his mother again for a long time. He couldn't forgive her for what she had done. There's no way his dad would have hit her, and he didn't understand why she kept saying he did. If she had just stopped nagging all of the time, his dad would never have left in the first place and everything would be fine. The boy would still have his own bedroom with his Narnia books and Nirvana posters, and he wouldn't have to walk so far to school every day, and he could just go and see his friends whenever he wanted.

She took all of that away from him.

CHAPTER 10

David liked to visit famous suicide spots. Beachy Head was his favourite. There are around twenty suicides at Beachy Head every year. The popular tourist spot has its own dedicated chaplaincy team patrolling the cliff edges, ready to pounce on anybody looking suspiciously morose. The local council even banned family members of so-called 'jumpers' from leaving shrines on the cliffs to their loved ones, for fear of encouraging others to follow suit.

David liked to peer over the edge into the rocky abyss below to see if he could feel anything for the recently deceased.

Nothing.

They chose to take the easy route out of whatever problems they had to deal with.

Weak.

If he managed to get lucky, sometimes David would spot a potential jumper hovering on the precipice. He would attract the attention of the chaplaincy team over to himself with a sufficiently sorrowful glance before they noticed the *real* jumper in time.

David sees all life as a test – you pass or you fail.

CHAPTER 11

For a case to go to trial at Crown Court in England there are many stages of evidence and procedure to go through first, often taking months and months of painstaking planning and preparation. This process is made more complicated by having numerous different agencies involved, each with their own agenda and priorities. The police just want the suspect charged, convicted and locked away in prison as quickly as possible. Of course, there have to be checks and balances on this, so the Crown Prosecution Service review every single piece of evidence before they are prepared to let this happen. Evidence does not just fall from trees like on TV; it takes time to collect it properly, and the police are the errand-boys sent off to gather it. Then the solicitor for the defence wants to review everything available so they can find a way to get their client off the hook. The police aren't allowed to hand anything directly to the defence, so everything has to go through the CPS, who are rather prone to losing things and blaming the police. Finally, when the numerous hearings and adjournments to allow the CPS more time have all passed, the barristers for both sides need to review everything so they can prepare to present their client's case at trial.

David always admired the prosecution barristers the most. To him they were like the rock stars of the criminal justice system, just breezing in the day of a trial and barking orders at everybody wheeling along their encyclopaedias of legal knowledge behind them. Their Russell Group law degrees and Inns-of-Court pupillages bestowing upon them an air of self-righteous superiority over everybody else. Then off for lunch with the judge and defence barrister. All very cosy, David thought.

The problem with this rather arduous process is the poor old victim is often forgotten about. He or she sits at home having poured out their heart and soul over some horrific experience they've had to endure, waiting for a phone call to tell them what day to turn up and sit around for hours waiting in court. It all just becomes a legal game of 'whodunnit' for the police, CPS, defence and prosecution – names on case files are just for filing; they don't actually *mean* anything any more. Maybe one day, after the hours of counselling and cognitive behavioural therapy have failed to erase the damage, the evidence is found to be lacking by some unconnected bureaucrat. A curt, professional 'thank you for reporting this matter, unfortunately we are unable to proceed' letter drops through the victim's letterbox and that's the end of it. From a victim's perspective, the system is fucked.

It's hard for people to turn up for work every day if you don't really have faith in the system. But not for David. For David, the fact a case would take so long to ever get to trial, if at all, didn't matter. For him, the thrill of the job came in those initial stages of first reporting, when the victim is all raw and exposed and humiliated. Ready to be caught on tape and endlessly replayed in David's mind. That's what got him motivated every day as he tried to *feel* something for somebody. Pity. Compassion. Empathy. Sympathy. *Anything*.

'David, sit down. There have been some concerns raised.'

Concerns. He fucking hated that word. In police parlance this had joined the lexicon of the utterly meaningless, along with 'inappropriate', 'unprofessional' and 'not a team player'. To David, these words all meant the same thing. They don't like what you do or the way you do it but there's no rule to say you're doing anything wrong, so instead we have these bullshit chats to make sure you understand that we don't like whatever it is you're doing. But there's nothing we can do about it.

'Oh, really? I'm sorry to hear that,' he lied as he sat in the pokiest inspector's office he'd ever seen.

One of those rooms so small one person has to stand up to allow someone else enough room to leave. A glorified fucking broom cupboard.

The unit was run by a detective inspector, with the assistance of a detective sergeant to run each team of four or five constables. At least on paper this is how it was supposed to work. The reality was everything had to meet the approval of the 'old sweats' who'd been there since the beginning of time. Like since around the time the Bow Street Runners morphed into Sir Robert Peel's so-called 'Peelers' in 1829 and thus the beginning of the first organised police force in the developed world. Some of those fuckers still called the shots from beyond the grave, David often thought. It didn't matter how efficient or good an idea might seem, to meet the approval of the *fascisti* it shouldn't deviate from the Golden Rule – 'this is the way it's always been done.'

The DI was a decent guy. A graduate, so rare in these parts, he possessed a worldlier view than the typical plod governor. He could recognise a critical mindset might be an asset, might be something to harness and nurture, not something to suppress. The *fascisti* disagreed. There was an order, a way of doing things that could never be tampered with because therein lies madness, they believed. These fucking hypocrites sat behind desks so old and weathered they made the occupant seem youthful, seething and simmering as the world evolved leaving them permanently out of touch and in complete denial at the same time. David had trouble fitting in.

'Colette says you didn't look into her case thoroughly enough.'

That fucking Medusa again, trying to turn *everything* she looked at to stone. Not content with putting her partner through the ringer, whoring out her children to the highest bidder of sympathy and wasting David's valuable time completely, it seemed she still wasn't satisfied.

'I don't see what more I could have done, sir,' David replied, at least half-truthfully.

He knew this couldn't be it. There was some hidden agenda as always. This was just the appetiser to try and unsettle him, to push him on the back foot before the yorker came through. That case was bullshit from the beginning, and they all knew it. The simpering wretch of a DS sat there scrawling some kind of hieroglyph down on paper as the DI spoke. All part of the game.

'Some feel as though you didn't show much compassion for the mother in this case. You understand how important it is to show compassion to our victims, don't you, David?'

Some feel. Not *I feel.* The difference may be slight to some but to David it was a fucking crevasse. So he wasn't sitting talking to the DI with his minion taking notes. He was being tried in the court of public opinion or more specifically, the opinion of the *fascisti* sitting crunching their bacon fries loudly in the office next door. David never felt the need to pretend to show compassion towards anyone. Mostly because he had no compassion for anyone. Ever. You are born alone in the world and you will die alone, he thought.

'She wasn't the alleged victim in this case, sir, the children were.'

David knew how this would now play out. He had refused to play along with their little game of pretending something was true when it wasn't true just to placate the egos of all those who had gone whining to the DI about him.

'That's not the point, David. You should be polite and professional to all victims and witnesses, and you know that.' The DI's tone shifted to mild irritation that David wasn't playing the game properly.

David just nodded. In his mind, he had won and that's all that mattered. The conversation which began with some drivel about compassion had now shifted to politeness and professionalism, which was the real agenda. We don't like that you're different to us, David. We need you to pretend you don't see through people's bullshit like the rest of us. That's all he heard, anyway. He wasn't really listening any more.

'And one more thing before you go, David,' the DI added.

Just one more thing. Fucking Columbo has arrived at the scene. Another tactic to unsettle you. You think you're through the awkward bit and you're about to get up and shake hands and smile and pretend you've taken on board what was said then they hit you with a *doosra* out of nowhere.

'I note that you've booked out the Clare interview DVD from the evidence room for viewing twelve times in the past month.'

The DI let the statement just hang there, no question implied or intended. He searched David's face for any signs of denial or embarrassment. There were none.

'That is correct,' came the blunt, slightly unnerved, response.

'My understanding is this case is now closed, David. I think you've done enough work on this one for now.'

Message received. Another statement left hanging in the slightly-damp air of the creaking old building the Met saw fit to base them all in. He nodded his acknowledgement and returned to his coffee-stained desk in the main office which suddenly became a hub of activity as the *fascisti* all pretended to be busy doing something.

Wankers, David thought to himself.

CHAPTER 12

Getting served was a big deal for any teenager. A *rite-du-passage* if you will. Walking in there trying to act as casual as possible hoping to avoid the total shame of being asked to produce ID. Better to start small and work his way up, the boy thought. Word gets around a small town pretty fast, and it so happened that the one off-licence where *everybody* in his year could get served was fairly close to his dad's flat. John's off-licence. John was probably so grateful for the custom he didn't really give a shit about the boy's age, but times were different back then.

A significant advantage the boy had over other boys in his year, apart from being the oldest, was that he no longer had the inconvenience of a parent at home to keep an eye on him any more. He could pretty much do what he wanted. The world was his oyster. And that evening the oyster in question was a single can of Special Brew. Better to start small and work his way up.

He'd spent several hours that day after getting home from school making the usual phone calls to various agencies – benefits, housing, council tax – that he was expected to make most days, pretending to be his dad. His dad insisted. It was better if the boy learned these things for himself. How to scam money out of the government. How to get stuff for free without contributing. Valuable lessons in life.

Eventually he had time to start looking through his dad's wardrobe for the right outfit for the evening's mission. He selected what he thought old people wore for such an occasion – smart jeans, collared-shirt, waistcoat, loads of aftershave. This is how people dressed for the off-licence, right? Shoes were a problem – his dad was a short-arse and wore a much smaller size than the boy. He often wondered how they were related at all; they bore no physical resemblance to each other whatsoever. His school Kickers would have to do; they were all he had. Hopefully he'd be in and out of there so fast his shoes wouldn't even be noticed anyway.

You might think this was some sort of special occasion. A birthday. A friend's party. Some sort of get-together. None of the above. This was purely about proving to everybody at school that he *could*. All his mates had been served there so he couldn't be the only one. Peer pressure is important to fourteen-year-old boys. As darkness smothered the evening, the boy made his way to the shop. The house of booze. The place where he would lose his beer-cherry. John seemed surprised to have a customer at all, peering over his reading glasses at the boy from his newspaper. Shopkeepers must be the most well-informed people on the planet, the boy often wondered – they spend the whole day reading the news. Must need to be really sharp to get anything past them, he thought. Good job he wore the aftershave, definitely makes him look older.

'Can of Special Brew, please.'

'Just the one?'

'Yes, please.'

The boy regretted saying please twice. Made him seem younger. Adults weren't usually so polite when they spoke to other adults, especially his dad. He never said please to anyone.

'That'll be 89p.'

Things were a lot cheaper back then in the post-industrial wasteland that South Yorkshire had become. The boy near-enough threw a pound coin across the counter; he was so eager to get the transaction over with.

'You're eighteen, aren't you?'

Damn. His eagerness must have given him away. Shit. Should have worn the checked shirt, the boy thought to himself.

'Yeah, of course I fucking am.'

This was a gamble. A massive gamble that could have backfired spectacularly. John seemed like a harmless old man, no threat whatsoever. But the boy had seen his dad get his own way by swearing at people loads of times. He knew it wasn't very nice or polite – he'd never swear at his maths teacher like that – but at that moment he didn't give a fuck. He just wanted that can of Special Brew.

'Take it and don't come back here,' said John wearily, like he'd been sworn at by a thousand kids and it just washed over him like water off a duck's back.

The boy didn't care. He snatched the can and was half-way up the street before anyone could even think about stopping him. He thought about saying 'keep the change' as he left but decided that would sound cheesy. He'd never heard his dad say that to anyone, mainly because his dad was a tight bastard and would have probably disowned him for leaving 11p behind. Five minutes later he was back at home, carefully placing his dad's clothes back in the exact same position in the wardrobe. He didn't want to risk opening the can yet in case it sprayed out all over his dad's shirt. Then there would have been hell to pay. Better to change first.

The boy savoured the fruits of his labour, slowly sipping the disgusting brown ale for the rest of the evening. How do people drink this, he wondered? Just wait until he told his mates at school tomorrow. Best not to drink it too quickly, he was no alcoholic.

Better to start small and work his way up.

CHAPTER 13

Kath had been on the child abuse investigation team forever. One of those people David hated. Boastful of the fact that she had sat in the same dog-eared swivel-chair for most of her working life, unashamed of the lack of progression in her career. A thirty-year constable, too afraid to ever seek promotion for fear that her inadequacies might be exposed to the rest of the *fascisti*. Better to just sit still. These were the kind of people that ran small departments in the Met, unofficially of course. Everything had to meet their approval and this included new additions to the staff. David was supposed to play the game, pander to her every whim and seek approval at every opportunity, earnestly hopeful that she might acknowledge his contribution to the team with a polite smile or, better still, a kind word.

David had a simple take on respect. He respected people who were effective at their job and didn't spend their days 'swinging the lead' talking about how good at their job they were. He respected people who stoically just got on with the job in hand and didn't look to palm-off their menial tasks to other people. He respected people who followed the rules, who didn't think they were special. Nobody is special. He respected people who treated him as an equal. Kath did not fall into this category and this set the tone of their relationship from day one. Also, she reminded him too much of his mother. Whiney. Northern. Always right.

David always remembered the advice of his A-level politics teacher, that the wise man knows the right questions to ask, not necessarily the right answer. The Met does not like people who ask questions. They are the police, they do the asking. You do the sit-down-with-your-fucking-mouth-shut.

We'll tell you when you can ask a question.

Never.

The way any briefing or training session officially ended in the Met was when the person leading the session would say 'any questions?' This actually meant 'thank you for sitting with your mouth shut, now you can go.' And everybody would file out of the room quietly. David picked this up fairly early on but never fully reconciled himself to it internally.

David had to be more careful now that he was on the DI's radar. He couldn't endlessly play Clare's interview back to himself any more and had to make do with the transcript he had in his desk drawer, hidden under some other paperwork like a copy of *Penthouse* magazine. Forbidden fruit. He knew it more or less word-for-word by now. He didn't need the executive summary.

His penis.

My anus.

Nine years old.

Alleyway.

Uncle.

Dead.

David knew all the facts he needed. The uncle spent his entire life living with what he'd done to his niece but never saw the utter carnage he had caused. He'd never see her trembling, broken, empty shell of a body sitting before him, re-telling every disgusting detail, pain etched in every corner of her face. Thanks to his death, no courtroom jury would ever see it either.

That was for David's eyes only.

What David may have lacked in experience on the department, he made up for in efficiency. He quickly learned to spot the cases that were going nowhere, that had no proper victim that could ever testify in court. His job was to dispense of these as quickly as possible in order to focus on the hidden gems like Clare. The ones he could savour every minute of. There were plenty of Colettes out there, David realised. Lots of angry, disenchanted women for whom no level was too low to stoop when it came to getting what they wanted. False accusations. Reputations in tatters. Lives ruined. All because of some angry cunt with daddy issues.

Kath saw things differently. Every victim deserves a chance to be heard, she would say. She'd single-handedly written all of the training manuals and she had all the experience, she would say. She didn't like the way David treated these women who just made things up to ruin men's lives. It probably wasn't their fault they lied. Maybe they were pushed to fabricate lies about someone. Maybe if they had been loved a little bit more as a child, they wouldn't be such a fuck-up later in life.

Total victim care. Every time David turned out to be right, it didn't matter. He should still be wasting his energy on these poor, insufferable women. It was all about the poor women, she would say.

Words were had with hen-pecked supervisors who knew who really called the shots in the small-office environment. Things were escalated. Dossiers were kept of David's every movement, every action or perceived inaction. Sob story after sob story was told in his presence, in some vain hope he could acquire more sympathy for these wretched women through some kind of osmosis. David would detach himself, just the way he had been taught.

Create distance.

Use cover.

Transmit.

He immersed himself deeper in Sally's suicide diary. How she came to hate her vagina as it brought her so much pain day after day, year after year. How this would make her choose to end her life in such a uniquely brutal and intimate way. He lost himself in Clare's interview transcript. Born on the wrong side of the wall, cries for help unacknowledged and unheard. People outside of this little world he had created for himself could teach him nothing, he supposed.

Create distance.

Eventually, the inevitable happened.

'David, there have been some concerns raised,' sighed the DI wearily.

'Oh, really. Who have I upset this time?'

'We think perhaps you need a mentor, somebody who has been doing this kind of work for a long time. Is there anybody here you think you can learn from?'

David shrugged his shoulders and said nothing. He saw the trap that had been set. Admit to needing help and they were vindicated in all their efforts to undermine him. Deny needing help and he was an arrogant prick who thought he knew better than everyone. Better to say nothing and let them make up their own minds.

'There must be somebody?' The DI persisted, hoping the awkward decision would be made for him.

Still nothing. For six months he had worked his cases, clearing out more rubbish more quickly than *anyone* in the department. His ability to see through bullshit and detect a genuine victim second to none. As it turns out, there aren't that many. But this wasn't how the game was supposed to be played. He was supposed to procrastinate, furrow his brow and seem to struggle to cope with it all. To be overwhelmed by the alleged sadness, to not see the lies and deceit until he was *told* to see the lies and deceit. By somebody on a higher pay grade than him.

It must be because he lacked experience, they'd assumed.

'Well, I was thinking about pairing you with Kath,' the DI eventually broke the silence.

'That won't work,' came his defiant response, instant this time.

'Why not?'

Because I fucking hate that woman? Because she represents everything that is wrong with this department, everything that is wrong about the fucking police in general? Because if you pair me with her every day, I will rip out her fucking throat and shit down her neck by the end of the week. These were the initial responses that flashed through David's mind.

'We have very different ways of working,' he politely offered instead.

'I've been on the department six months,' he continued. 'I've had no complaints about my work rate or case management, apart from a few women think I'm too mean to them. To give me a mentor at this stage would suggest you should have given me one earlier, rather than wait six months before doing anything about it. Nobody else has a mentor so you would be singling

68

me out for special treatment, despite a lack of any formal disciplinary or capability proceedings against me. I note that a Police Federation representative has not been invited to this meeting. I respectfully urge you to reconsider, sir.'

Use cover.

David had rehearsed this, knowing which buttons to push at the right time. Mentioning the Federation made him inwardly chuckle to himself – they were fucking useless. Fat fucks whose sole contribution to improving police pay and conditions was a big knees-up every autumn by the seaside at each member's expense, regaling each other with war stories and the 'good old days'. When called into action their standard advice was to be a good boy, toe the line, do what he say, do what he say. A blancmange on the chair next to him would have more impact on the outcome.

But this was how the game was played.

The DI contemplated David's carefully-crafted response for a few moments. He didn't really have a problem with David; they actually got along quite well on a personal level. They both read books from time to time, which set them apart from the rest of the *fascisti*. But certain appearances had to be made. The rest of the team found David difficult to work with so it fell to him to try and resolve it. Like he wasn't busy enough.

'OK, David, I only said I was considering it. Nothing is decided.'

It was true, he had given himself that wiggle-room from the outset. But David's speech had the desired effect. He created enough doubt and raised a few questions that might later have to be addressed. The DI could do without the headache, he thought. Just run along and play nicely, he may as well have said. They had to be seen to be offering support, but there had to be a genuine professional reason for doing so. Not just the whim of some menopausal old sweat throwing her teddies out of the pram. David doubted that she would have been much pleased with working so closely alongside him anyway; their antipathy was mutual. This was the Met Police book-of-management-skills way of dealing with the situation; to make the potential outcome less appealing for all parties than the current status quo. That way, people tend to complain less in future.

Kath kept her fucking mouth shut for a while after that meeting.

Transmit.

CHAPTER 14

The boy shivered in the cold winter night. His dad's car wasn't the warmest place to spend the night, the windows steaming quickly as his warm breath instantly met with temperatures rapidly pushing below zero. He hadn't really had time to plan this; he had no blankets, no means to keep himself warm. The back seat of his dad's battered old Ford Escort estate wasn't long enough for him to stretch out at all, but it was slightly softer than lying in the boot. It was three a.m. He was cold and tired. But he didn't cry.

Eight hours earlier the boy was inside his dad's flat playing his guitar. It was an Encore copy of the classic Sunburst Fender Stratocaster shape used by Kirk Hammett from Metallica, amongst many others. Obviously, his version was a little cheaper in build and quality than what Kirk might be accustomed to, but we all have to start somewhere, the boy figured. His dad had wanted to get him this horrible purple guitar which was about twenty pounds cheaper in the second-hand shop they went to, but for once the boy managed to convince his dad to part with a little more cash, seeing as it was

Christmas and all. The boy wasn't a particularly good guitar player, but he wanted to get better. And the only way to do that was to keep practising, the guy in the guitar shop had told him.

'Stop making that racket, you're shit,' were his dad's typically warm and supportive words.

The boy had learned not to expect praise from his dad any more. His younger brother was falling further and further down the downward spiral, and his dad just seemed angry all of the time. His brother had been permanently expelled from three schools by the age of thirteen for things like hitting teachers and bringing drugs onto school premises.

It wasn't his fault; his mum would always say. It was the teacher's fault. They all had it in for him, she would insist.

His dad thought beating him harder might solve the problem. It didn't.

Eventually, his mum decided his brother needed a fresh start somewhere else and moved back up to the North East where she grew up, taking his brother with her. The boy was glad. He didn't speak to his mum or brother anymore anyway.

'I need you out of here tonight, Karin is staying over,' the boy's dad told him with a fixed glare.

'I don't have anywhere to go, I haven't made any plans,' the boy offered hopefully.

'Tough shit. Make some plans. Don't come back here tonight.'

By now the boy was out drinking fairly regularly most weekends. It was a small town up north. There wasn't a great deal else to do. He used to do loads of things every evening when he lived with his mum and dad together. On Mondays and Thursdays, he did karate. Tuesdays and Fridays was scouts. Wednesdays was football training. Sometimes he had a football tournament or karate competition at the weekends. He was good at karate, especially doing the *kata* forms. He won loads of trophies and certificates for *kata,* which was all about memorising a set routine of moves and executing it perfectly for the judges. Everything in the correct order, he was good at that. He wasn't so great at fighting. He found it too unpredictable.

The boy knew that he could get served at most pubs in the area by now, but he hadn't had a chance to borrow any of his dad's clothes that evening to make him look older so he was just going to have to chance it. For a small town of about twenty thousand people, there were loads of pubs everywhere, as if people around here had nothing else to do except drink and moan about some woman called Margaret Thatcher. Apparently, she took away all of their jobs, but the boy wondered if that was true, how come they could all still afford to sit in the pub most days.

73

He made his way down to the Coach and Horses where pretty-much everybody was underage so he got served, no problem. Years later they were shut down for serving minors and it turned into an Indian restaurant. Bit of diversity needed in the area, apparently.

He didn't really have a plan. He couldn't exactly just invite himself round to someone's house to spend the night. He didn't have much money and hadn't even planned to be out, so he had to drink really slowly to make his pints last longer. He could take his beer now, he was used to it.

The night dragged on. It was early January; everybody was skint. Not many people were out, another reason he hadn't planned anything. The bell rang for last orders, and the boy just wandered around the cold, dark streets for ages. He did get invited to a party at somebody's house but he didn't really know them, and they were a lot older than him. They said they had loads of booze and drugs at the house; he could have whatever he liked if he went with them. The boy had never really taken any drugs. He didn't see the point and never understood why people would trust a tablet from a complete stranger. His mum had mistakenly fed him a sterilising tablet when he was young once; he had to have his stomach pumped out at hospital and he nearly died. His mum said she thought it was a paracetamol. Since then the boy didn't really trust any tablets he was given by other people.

The boy thought the people having the party seemed a bit dodgy so he didn't go. Why would they just randomly invite along a boy half their age, he wondered? He remembered reading about another boy called Ben who lived not far from them who disappeared on holiday in Greece. His parents never saw him again. The boy thought to himself his dad would probably be pleased if that happened to him, then Karin could come and stay over whenever she wanted.

The boy was running out of options. His dad had always told him not to go to strangers' houses. But then his dad had told him not to go home that night either. Then he remembered his dad's car passenger door didn't lock properly. He'd be able to sleep in there and then just walk in tomorrow morning as if he spent the night at a friend's house. His dad never bothered asking where he'd stayed out anyway. Good job they didn't have a nice car like his friend Tim whose dad just got a brand-new Vauxhall Vectra. Tim's parents were really nice. They always used to give the boy a lift home at night if he went around to their house to make sure he was safe. Tim was really lucky, the boy thought to himself.

Sure enough, the passenger door opened and the boy climbed into the back seat. It was freezing cold and uncomfortable but eventually he managed to fall asleep. A few hours later he was woken by a police officer standing next to the car, tapping on the car window.

Somebody had seen him climb into the back seat and reported it to the police.

'Can you tell me why you're sleeping in this car, young man?'

The officer's voice was friendly; he seemed more concerned than annoyed. The boy thought quickly what to say. He couldn't say that his dad had kicked him out for the night. Then the police would knock on his dad's door and wake him up, and the boy would get in loads of trouble once the police left. He couldn't say that he had just tried any car door, then they would think he was trying to nick cars. Some of the people in his year at school used to brag about nicking cars all the time. They didn't come in to school very often any more.

'I live here. I lost my keys so thought I'd just sleep in here tonight, that's all.' The boy nervously indicated towards the flat as he spoke.

The male officer spoke to the female officer he was with for a few minutes and then talked into his radio for a bit. The boy just sat in the car waiting. He remembered worrying that he was going to get into loads of trouble when his dad found out about this. But it wasn't his fault. The boy didn't understand what else he was supposed to do. The police officers seemed really kind. He heard one say to the other 'no signs of forced entry' or something like that. They asked for his name and how old he was. The boy told them the truth.

He thought at least if he got arrested, he would have somewhere warm to sleep that night.

'I think you need to go inside your house now. It's not safe for you sleeping out here at your age.' The female officer spoke to him this time. She had a really soft, kind voice.

The boy had told them he had lost his keys. Even though they were in his pocket, he knew he could get into trouble for lying to the police. And he had been drinking underage so he could get into even more trouble. He agreed to go inside.

The officers knocked at his dad's flat and spoke to the boy's dad for a few minutes. The boy was really cold by now and started shivering. His dad looked really angry at first when he saw the boy stood with two police officers, but then when they explained to him what had happened, he seemed really embarrassed and kept thanking them for bringing him home safe.

'Fucking hypocrite,' the boy thought to himself.

The boy spent the rest of the night on the sofa, warm at last. He kept thinking how kind the police officers had been to him. His dad was always moaning about the police saying they were pigs. Which didn't make any sense because his dad was obsessed with pigs. There were framed pictures of pigs all over the flat. In the morning, his dad never mentioned anything about the night before. In fact, they never spoke of it again.

CHAPTER 15

First thing to do once a case was allocated to you was to work out your investigation strategy and show that you had done this on the crime report. Accountability. Arse-covering. If you say you were going to do something, it was as good as doing it. If you say you planned to move the heavens and the earth in order to find an outstanding suspect, they were as good as found. But this problem was rare in the child abuse world because the suspects were most often well-known to the alleged victim and usually living in the same house as them.

Because you don't get to choose your family. They are allocated to you.

David preferred to work alone. He had a system that played to his strengths and minimised exposure of his weaknesses. The Standard Operating Procedures insist everything should be done in pairs for officer safety reasons, until there weren't enough staff. Then the Standard Operating Procedures didn't give a fuck about your safety. David figured he was a big boy; he could handle himself. Most nonces are generally not noted for their excellent fighting skills. If it was convenient for the job to send him out alone when it suited them, he figured it was convenient for him the rest of the time too. He didn't need anybody else's help.

One of the reasons David had first moved to London was the sheer diversity of the populace he would eventually serve. He grew up in a small northern town, one road in and one road out. Zero diversity. Everybody from the same place, worked at the same steelworks, drank at the same pubs, kids went to the same school. In the north they call this 'community' but to David it was too much, too claustrophobic. Everybody in each other's pockets, everybody knowing each other's business. He longed for the anonymity the metropolis offered and took full advantage of it.

He certainly wasn't here in the big city to make friends. People couldn't be relied upon.

What struck David about London when he first arrived was how close to each other the rich and poor lived, often along the same street. Massive Georgian townhouses worth millions opposite dingy red-brick council estates with burnt-out cars and old mattresses littered about the place. He found it fascinating. You didn't need to wonder how the other half lived. You could just look out of the window and see for yourself.

London had poverty like he'd never really seen before, but it had riches beyond his wildest expectations in equal measure. Take the Evans family for example. Large townhouse near the tube in central London. Large country house in Kent. Holiday home in Switzerland, handy for Lake Geneva during summer and the Alps for skiing in winter. Mummy is a writer and spends her time between the three houses. Daddy only appears at weekends, spending most of his time in the City earning the big bucks. Two lovely young children need a nanny, of course.

Somebody has to look after them.

It always struck David how the richer people were, the less time they spent with their own children. As though childcare was too menial a task for them and should be delegated to some poor immigrant nanny. These were the people who took full advantage of the common market.

A succession of young female nannies from Eastern Europe joined the Evans household as paid employees. Mr Evans fucked all of them.

In the marital bed. In the kitchen. In the bathroom. In London. In Kent. In Switzerland. Any opportunity he got really. Mrs Evans was not amused. He barely even bothered to conceal the affairs, as if he wanted her to know the consequences of bringing another woman into the household. Betrayed, humiliated, shamed – she hatches a plan of pure genius. She can't possibly throw him out, far too embarrassing. What would the neighbours say? As Mr Evans seems determined to fuck every *female* that enters the household, what better than a gay *male* nanny instead – maybe that will stop his errant ways, she hoped.

The nanny in question hailed from Spain. It seemed the Evans had had their fill of former Eastern bloc countries for now, time to try sunnier climes. Roberto arrived. Mrs Evans delighted with herself – a more tactile, camp and extravagant gay man you could not hope to meet, she boasted to her upper middle-class friends over afternoon tea. Roberto is introduced to everybody with gleaming smiles all round by Mrs Evans. This should do the trick, she thought.

Roberto was great with the kids, at first. Until he started fucking them.

Five-year-old boy and seven-year-old girl in equal measure. In London. In Kent. In Switzerland. Any opportunity he got really. It wasn't always fully penetrative, but it was sometimes. In fact, the only person *not* getting any action in this twisted household of iniquity was poor Mrs Evans, David wondered to himself.

Eventually Roberto is outed and on the next plane to Spain, duly returned and dragged off the tarmac at Gatwick by David. There was no misery for him to take any pleasure in here; this man was a monster, a predator of the worst kind. A very well-paid predator who had been brought into the home by a very wealthy family.

David blamed the parents. It was always the parents. They fuck you up.

They put their children at such risk because they didn't want the inconvenience of spending too much time raising them. Parents who wanted for nothing and could provide everything in the end provided only suffering of the worst kind imaginable.

Those children fucked for life by a double-betrayal. David pondered the utter senselessness of it all over a large glass, after seeing Roberto led down to the cells from the dock earlier that afternoon. He had developed a *penchant* for fine French brandy. As they peered across the street at the have-nots, those two young Evans children growing up would have expected to see the lion's share of suffering in that street take place over there.

Across the street.

In the other place.

The place with all the poor people.

Not in their perfect little world of ski trips and country houses.

David downed the contents of his glass and replenished them quickly, as he sank deeper into despair.

CHAPTER 16

'If you're in a bad situation, don't worry it'll change.
If you're in a good situation, don't worry it'll change.'
[John A Simone Sr, American writer and broadcaster]

Things had begun to settle down and improve for the boy around the time his final year of school began. The council had finally relented and given them a bigger house; he had his own room again. His mother and brother were both out of the picture, having moved away. Even though his dad still wasn't around much, the boy was used to this by now and knew how to look after himself. He could survive on just one meal per day now, usually something meagre he ate at school. The new house was much closer to school as well so he didn't have to walk too far again.

The boy continued to excel in most subjects, especially English and French. He didn't really have to try very hard to do well, he thought; it was all quite easy. He wasn't really part of any one particular social group. He preferred to straddle the divide and got along fairly well with the nerds, the metal-heads, the boys on the football team, the popular girls, the less-popular girls.

He didn't really feel part of any one group but he preferred it that way. The highlight of the school year was always the annual day trip to Alton Towers, where the boy remembers some frantic fingering taking place on the coach. Her name was Kate, but after taking four of the boy's fingers inside her, she was forever known as KitKat thereafter.

Children can be cruel.

Nine GCSEs achieved without too much effort, slightly less impressive than he had hoped, but the boy went on to college to study his A-levels, having breezed through school without ever really applying himself. During one particular lesson when asked a question by the teacher, the boy thought if he stayed very still, the teacher might not notice that his left hand was currently stroking the *labia majora* of the lucky girl sitting next to him.

'You won't find the answer down there, boy.' His plan was foiled by a rather observant business studies teacher.

His grandmother died when he was sixteen. Unbeknown to the boy, she had been living on borrowed time for ten years after a previous heart attack, but nobody ever told the boy this. She died suddenly aged sixty-three which the boy would come to realise was no age to go.

She was a formidable woman in every sense of the word. Always in control of everybody and everything.

Always looked out for the boy, always keen for him to do well at school and make something of himself. Always gave his dad a hard time for leaving the boy alone so often, not that he ever listened.

When she died, the boy lost the only person he thought really understood him. His grandfather always wanted the best for him but was prone to seeing only what he wanted to see and ignoring what he didn't. She wasn't like everybody else. She didn't always tell him that he should be nice to his brother or speak to his mother again. She let him be, let him grow into his own person with his own reasons for not wanting to do certain things.

When Karin got pregnant, his grandmother was furious, telling his dad that he should be focussing on the children he already had and not starting a new family with somebody else. He didn't listen.

Everything changed. As the dominant matriarch of the family, his grandmother had held the family together in a way only women of that Blitz generation could. His grandfather was forever broken after she passed. His dad looked for something new to replace the mother he lost and found it with a new baby and a new family elsewhere.

Then his brother came back. Not content with having kicked one son out of her home a few years earlier, his mother now sent his younger brother back down the A1 in similar circumstances. Unable to settle at school. Turning increasingly violent at home towards her. Excluded from every school he ever set foot in, the younger sibling was out of control.

And now he was his dad's problem, his mother said.

To be fair, she had a point. His dad had spent the last two years sending letter after letter to his younger son saying he 'belonged in Yorkshire' and he would make sure he came back one day. Hardly words likely to help to settle an angry, confused teenager seething with rage at the entire world.

His dad had to be at home a lot more often now. This was unbearable for both him and the boy. They had grown apart and weren't used to being around each other so often. Like in a marriage of convenience where each party spends the minimal amount of time in each other's company as possible. Add into the mix a younger sibling who was either at home stealing anything not nailed down or out selling said items for drugs, the environment was completely toxic.

The boy's Sega Mega Drive, gone.

The boy's Sunburst Stratocaster-copy guitar, gone.

The boy's Honda scooter, gone.

The boy wondered why it was so important for his dad to be around now for his brother, but it hadn't seemed important when he was that age. Nobody ever answered that question for him.

His dad did not possess the parenting skills required to handle his brother. Nobody did. The boy witnessed some savage beatings. The horrible aura of violence and anger hung in the air constantly. The boy needed a way out, desperately.

There is something about witnessing a child being beaten that stays with you, forever.

The college provided a free counselling service. The boy wasn't afraid to seek help from strangers; it was family he shunned. Thus began a three-year relationship with anti-depressants that eventually took the boy away to another continent, as far away from home as he could possibly go. It would scupper any future hopes he had of joining the military and later leave him seeking the next best thing.

When you start taking anti-depressants, you hope it will just be a temporary fix. You search deep within yourself for the wherewithal to deal with things without chemical help. But for the boy, the search had yielded no results and time was running out. He needed to get through the next two years to get his A-levels, to go to university. Thanks to the sage advice of some good teachers, that was his way out. He didn't care about his brother. He just wanted to get out.

Two years passed. The longest two years of the boy's life. New siblings had arrived, one for each parent. One each to prove to the other how they'd moved on. A new perfect family for them both to start again. The boy never lived with either, never asked for either to exist. One sibling had already brought him enough hassle; he didn't need any more. In a rare conversation with his dad that didn't involve his brother in some way, the boy one day said:

'If I don't get the results I need for university, I'll probably kill myself.'

Not an easy thing for a parent to hear. He meant every word. The medication had helped balance things out, but that was always with the hope of light at the end of the tunnel, an escape route. If that was taken away, the walls would come crashing in around him, the boy thought. He'd visited all the universities he'd applied to by himself. His parents had no interest in such things. They were too interested in their new families.

The day arrived. The boy held the envelope nervously in his hand. So much pressure on this moment. He got the results he needed. He was finally leaving it all behind, on his terms. He sold what belongings his brother hadn't already taken and packed his clothes. No black bin-bags this time. The boy had no intention of coming home during the holidays; he had made sure he had accommodation for the full year. There was nothing to come back for.

One last visit to see his mother. Perhaps they could reconcile before he left. They'd had a few tentative visits the past year but nothing had been resolved. The resentment

still burned inside the boy like a fire, and his mother remained unrepentant. One last chance.

'I don't think you should go to university. You should stay here with me if you don't like being at your dad's any more,' his mother said, much to the boy's surprise.

'Why?'

'Well, Mike said he doesn't want to be with me anymore so I'm by myself now. I need someone to help me look after the baby.'

The baby she chose to have aged forty-three. The baby she chose to have with a fucking waste of space like Mike, his unwillingness for any meaningful commitment never hidden from anybody with half a brain in their head. More responsibility that the boy never asked for. No fucking way.

'Good bye, Mum.'

CHAPTER 17

There is something about seeing a dead baby that stays with you, forever.

Lying prostrate on the cold, grey hospital slab. All hope lost. No tubes or machines connected to the baby's organs any more. Life pronounced extinct. Sudden infant death syndrome (SIDS) – commonly known as 'cot death' – is the sudden, unexpected and unexplained death of an apparently healthy baby. In the UK, more than two hundred babies die suddenly and unexpectedly every year. Most deaths happen during the first six months of a baby's life. Infants born prematurely or with a low birthweight are at greater risk. SIDS also tends to be slightly more common in baby boys. SIDS usually occurs when a baby is asleep, although it can occasionally happen while they're awake. The exact cause of SIDS is unknown, but it's thought to be down to a combination of factors. Any unexplained death requires police investigation, the death of a defenceless infant especially. The occurrence of SIDS is thankfully rare, the sort of case a police officer might deal with once or maybe twice in their entire career.

The Ferreira family had travelled to London from Brazil. Not from any of the well-known cities, the family hailed from an obscure, remote part of the Amazon rainforest. They were essentially tribespeople on holiday. The mother still a child herself, aged sixteen. The young father and both his parents, they had all made the arduous ten-hour journey from the rainforest by bus and then onto the twelve-hour flight to London with three-week-old baby Felipe. They came to visit another relative living in London. They were barely off the plane and through immigration control before the baby started having breathing problems. They made it to the place they were staying in south London for the night but, tragically, Felipe did not make it through to the morning. Felipe died before the ambulance arrived; there was nothing the medical team could do.

When a baby dies in such unexplained circumstances, there are protocols and procedures to follow. Everything that has passed through the baby for the past twenty-four hours needs to be analysed, which means all baby formula and used nappies have to be gathered. The bedding the child last slept on is seized as a police exhibit, along with the clothing they wore and any toys or dummies that might have been ingested. Readings are taken of the baby's room temperature, all to establish that a safe environment had been provided prior to the baby's death.

In short, everything that the family have of their deceased infant is taken away from them at the most agonising time of their life.

David had never been so close to this level of pain and suffering before. The parents, absolutely inconsolable as you might expect. To add to the distress, none of the family spoke English, so an interpreter was thrust into the middle of that horrific situation to establish facts, a timeline, any signs the baby was unwell prior to being put to bed. David felt as sorry for the interpreter as he did for the family involved. At last, some humanity stirred within him. Some feeling awakened. When he got home later that evening, sometime in the middle of the night, he drowned himself in brandy. Anything to numb his sadness, to block out the image of the baby on the slab.

David had never been one to open up about his feelings. Allowing somebody in had always ended with him being very badly let down in the past, so David's defences were permanently up. Some mistook this for hostility, and this misperception then became a permanent barrier to good relationships. David figured he didn't owe anybody any explanation. That's just the way he was, and they had to accept it. Dealing with SIDS was an opportunity for David to show a softer side to his colleagues, to show that he did care and that he did not completely lack compassion. But these are not emotions and behaviours that can just be switched on. After years of having his defences up, David didn't even know how to lower the drawbridge any more.

'How are you feeling after yesterday, David,' one of his colleagues, Rachel, politely enquired.

'Fine.'

'We've all been through it. If you need to talk about it to anybody, we're all here,' she continued.

Rachel was being genuinely supportive and able to rise above the machismo of most of the *fascisti*. However, this was certainly not a line of questioning David was comfortable with and he prayed she would soon stop. He kept his responses short.

'I'm okay, thanks.'

It's not that he didn't want to talk about it. He didn't know how. Every year officers in the department were required to attend a psychological health screening. It was completely confidential but everybody understood the game. It was a classic Catch 22. Go in there and tell them you're feeling manically depressed about a SIDS case and you'd be back in uniform walking the beat before the door closed behind you. The Met had crafted yet another system whereby the consequences of complaining were less desirable than the status quo. So, you go in there and say everything is fine. Then you go home and hit the self-destruct button. Alcoholism and divorce featured very highly across the department. There were a lot of fathers who only saw their kids at weekends due to the toll the job had taken on their marriage.

David didn't have children. He figured there was already enough sadness in the world.

It was eventually established that there were no suspicious circumstances to baby Felipe's death. The incredibly long journey probably hadn't done him much good. Maybe he picked up some sort of infection along the way through the change in climate and atmospheric pressure. It was difficult to say for sure.

But David felt uncomfortable with what he had seen. Would you expect a parent to put their three-week-old baby through that journey? Perhaps it was a stretch to say they were deliberately negligent but, in David's mind, they were fucking stupid.

It was a terrible, unspeakable tragedy for the Ferreira family and a rare heartening experience for David that he could still feel something. But nothing made sense any more. For years David had survived on his wits with his defences firmly in place, feeling very little and therefore being affected by very little in return. He began to question if exposure to such immense sadness was beginning to affect him. Or was it his drinking habit, which was threatening to spiral out of control at any time. Amazing how the mind clouds judgement with the fog of alcohol.

He looked around for answers and found some comfort in the Bible. He had always found the notion of religion fascinating. The power of a set of ideas to compel thousands of people to behave in a certain way, to feel something with every fibre of their being and to hate something with equal zeal. Religion hadn't been talked about much at home, but the same applied to most topics beyond the football results and *Coronation Street*.

He couldn't blame his parents for this path along which he was about to embark. This was his alone. David took solace in the words he found, words written centuries ago yet seemingly so apt for the way he felt about the world.

'Do give heed to me, O LORD, And listen to what my opponents are saying! Should good be repaid with evil? For they have dug a pit for me. Remember how I stood before You To speak good on their behalf, So as to turn away Your wrath from them. Therefore, give their children over to famine And deliver them up to the power of the sword; And let their wives become childless and widowed. Let their men also be smitten to death, Their young men struck down by the sword in battle. May an outcry be heard from their houses, When You suddenly bring raiders upon them; For they have dug a pit to capture me And hidden snares for my feet. Yet You, O LORD, know All their deadly designs against me; Do not forgive their iniquity Or blot out their sin from Your sight. But may they be overthrown before You; Deal with them in the time of Your anger!'
(Jeremiah 18:19-23)

CHAPTER 18

The boy wasn't the first in his family to go to university; his older cousin had just pipped him to that honour by a couple of years. But there was no long history of academic success in the family to put any kind of pressure on the boy. His parents certainly had no real expectations for him, so he was at last able to just enjoy something for himself, away from everything he had fought so hard to distance himself from. For the first time he encountered middle-class children who had not been given *any* choice about whether they were going to university or not, the matter was simply not up for discussion in their household. The boy felt sorry for these young people, trapped by their parents' expectations and desire to keep up appearances at the golf club. In the first term he saw so many of these kids drop out, unable to cope away from home.

How weak, the boy thought to himself.

What the boy hadn't counted on was the hold anti-depressants had on his body by that stage. When he felt better away from all the problems of the past, he promptly stopped taking them. Which was a huge mistake, of course. As any doctor will advise, the dosage needs to be reduced gradually over time to ensure no relapse or sudden 'crash', which is exactly what happened to the boy. He was devastated to be so dependent on something, crushed that his new-found emotional freedom was being curtailed. It was as though the past remained very much there with him in the present, like an old friend he couldn't quite shake off. This life lesson was not lost on the boy.

The boy enjoyed his first year, made friends easily as most students thrust together in squalor and alcohol tend to do. But he still needed the medication to keep him on an even keel. An opportunity came along for him to spend his second year away in Canada on exchange, an opportunity he wasn't going to miss. Amazingly, by this age he hadn't even been to London yet and now here he was about to go and live on a different continent. A family holiday to Spain aside, he'd barely even been abroad. This was all due to his family holding him back, the boy told himself. Now that he was in control of his own destiny, he wouldn't be held back by anybody or anything.

As he packed his bag, he decided not to take the last of the anti-depressants away with him. His dosage had been gradually reduced over the past year, and the boy decided it was time to sink or swim on his own.

In Canada he settled in quickly and made friends easily. He shared an apartment with a Chinese-Canadian guy named Jon, who would become one of his closest friends. Jon was about five years older and so a little wiser. He seemed to feel sorry for the nervy, skinny English boy and took him under his wing.

The boy felt like he was growing as a person, experiencing new things and surviving on his own, just like he always knew he could. He never needed the medication again. He found other ways to stem the flow of despair.

Returning to England to complete his final year of study, the boy had barely seen or spoken to his parents in three years. The occasional phone call here and there, the boy consciously wanted to cut those ties early. He was on speaking terms with his mum now, but the relationship remained fractious, and there would follow a pattern of long periods of time with no contact with either parent in between occasional visits and phone calls for years to come.

The boy had little or no contact with his brother for most of the next ten years. Somehow it was easier for the boy to blame the toxic home environment on his little brother's criminal antics than it was to blame his parents' failure to handle it.

Both his parents moved away to different houses in new areas, so every last physical vestige of the boy's childhood was gone, existing only in his memory. Their new houses felt cold and alien to him, forming no part of his world any more.

The boy fell in love for the first time in his final year, a girl who lived in the same residential block called Jenny. She was everything he wasn't – outgoing, cheerful, positive and posh like all southerners, it seemed to the boy raised in the grim shadow of Thatcherism. She had a really close family and loved her siblings dearly. The boy enjoyed being a part of all of this, something he had never experienced before.

With the medication behind him and some global travel under his belt, the boy now felt he was leaving his past behind. They graduated together on the same day and decided to move to Cornwall together to work in a bar for the summer. By now the boy had been rejected by the army due to his history of depression, so he figured that he might as well enjoy his last summer of freedom before looking for a real job. They had a tiny little chalet together, spent the evenings working and most of the daytimes in bed or on the beach. For the few months it lasted it was bliss, not a care or responsibility in the world for either of them.

But the past wasn't completely behind him. He still couldn't bring himself to fully trust anybody. Jenny was still close with her ex-partner, and the boy couldn't handle this, fearful he would lose someone who meant so much to him. Convinced she might betray him, he cheated on her just to make sure he wouldn't be the one who got hurt first. It was a mistake. He ruined everything that night, and things fell apart with Jenny in the weeks that followed. She was a sweet and lovely person and never deserved what the boy did to her.

Jenny left.

Having distanced himself from his family and now having pushed away the only person he'd ever loved, the boy looked around for something to provide some semblance of order, meaning and structure to his life he so desperately needed.

In September 2002 the boy joined the Metropolitan Police Service.

CHAPTER 19

The word *fascist* as a pejorative came about following the defeat of Germany, Italy and Japan – the so-called 'Axis' – at the end of World War Two. George Orwell famously wrote in 1944 that even by then the term was almost entirely meaningless. Most English people, he went on to say, would happily accept the term *bully* as a valid synonym for *fascist*. As a political description, *fascist* has been variously hijacked and mis-applied since then by groups across the traditional left-right political spectrum, but as a term of social commentary, its common meaning as laid out by Orwell remains universally understood. Someone or something described as being *fascist* is a bully.

David sat seething in anger and frustration at the complete inaction of his supervisors. He'd heard it, they'd all heard it. Everyone burying their heads pathetically in their case files or computer screens, desperately hoping someone else would take the initiative. He could barely contain his anger. If somebody didn't act in an official way, he would tell her exactly what he thought of her in a very *unofficial* way.

'The Metropolitan Police Service takes all allegations of racism very seriously and strongly urges all staff to report any incidents they feel to be offensive in nature.' They could all recite the mantra as well as they could remember the police caution by now. *Institutionally racist*, MacPherson had branded an entire organisation following the collapse of the first Stephen Lawrence murder investigation. Thousands of officers unfairly tarred with the same brush, many of David's colleagues felt.

Things were supposed to have changed.

'David, it has been alleged that you have used derogatory racist language towards a colleague,' said the inspector in his office a few days later.

The words hit David like a cannonball. He was many things, but he was no racist.

'Oh, really? What exactly am I supposed to have said?'

'You referred to Tracey as *a fat jock cunt*.'

David couldn't quite believe he was hearing this. This was a new low, even for the *fascisti* he was forced to endure working alongside. He fucking hated Tracey, that he would never deny. She was another Kath in the making. Pig-fucking ignorant, barely able to read and write without using her finger to hover over each word. Some barely intelligible Glaswegian noise emanating from her fat fucking face every so often, usually to criticise something she didn't quite understand.

Like the alphabet.

Or the English language.

Or when it was acceptable to pepper most of her sentences with words like *chink*, *paki* or *nigger*.

To David, she belonged in the stone age along with Enoch Powell and the rest of the Flintstones. The sad fact was she was younger than he was, the future face of policing in the twenty-first century. David fucking despised her.

'Any update on my complaint about her, sir?'

He knew the answer. He should have known better. Create a situation where the outcome of raising an issue is less desirable than the status quo. This was textbook Met.

'I'm afraid not. Nobody else heard her call those people *chinks*. But they all heard you refer to her as *a fat jock cunt* the other day,' came the prepared response.

Fucking cowards. Weak to the core, every last one of them. Successfully drilled on the order of things – never complain about a colleague, even if they are useless racist fuckwit. So now a plan was quickly concocted to remove the complainant from the scenario, thus dealing with the problem. Nothing to see here.

Create distance.

Use cover.

Transmit.

'Are you suggesting the terms *jock* and *chink* are equally offensive, sir?'

'That is not the matter under discussion, David,' he deflected.

David said nothing more. He knew the outcome already. This was the beginning of the end for him on this particular team. Some nonsense about not being a team-player, he wasn't really listening any more.

For years this is what more-educated liberal-minded white officers are forced to endure. Sit there with your mouth shut while the *fascisti* spout off their racist bile.

Just accept it.

This is the way things are.

Things had moved on slightly. Ethnic officers very rarely endured this sort of bullshit any more post-MacPherson. But in a sad way, since that watershed it was *worse*. Now it was known and *understood* that this shit was offensive to some people, so best it was only said when the ethnic people aren't in earshot. It doesn't matter if your husband, wife, neighbour, friend or uncle happens to be ethnic – you're white so you just sit there and put up with it.

And don't even think about reporting it, or the consequences for *you* will be severe.

Progress indeed.

David was no snowflake. He despised excessive political correctness as much as the next person, but that didn't mean he wasn't sensitive to the feelings of oppressed minorities. He had always kept his Jewish heritage to himself. His personality was enough of a target for the *fascisti*, never mind handing them a fucking free hit with his ethnic heritage as well.

Be a good Jew and stay quiet.

Something else to thank his mother for.

Better to stand for one day than to spend a lifetime on your knees, thought David. The famous words of some Latin American revolutionary he believed, though he couldn't quite remember which one. He had his principles, and they could never take that away from him. He didn't give a fuck about being a team player or being privy to any of their inbred white-trash small-minded nonsense. He was no paragon of tranquillity and virtue. He hated plenty of people for plenty of reasons. But he'd sooner have scrotal electrolysis than be an accomplice to racism.

CHAPTER 20

He kept turning the events of the previous evening over and over in his mind. The cold, sterile hospital corridors. The detached staff going about their business. Felipe lying motionless on the emergency room table, life extinguished. His mother beside herself in grief, all colour drained from her adolescent face. The horror that unfolded right before their eyes that morning after such a long, tiring journey the previous day. Felipe's final journey.

Is this what it took for him to feel something, the boy began to wonder. Numb for so long, was something deep within him finally finding sustenance in Felipe's tragic demise? He had seen countless tragedies, seen some of the worst pain imaginable. Nothing. Unmoved. Only now was he beginning to see what other people saw every time they read a sad story or turned over to see the news on TV that particular day.

Had he really been so self-centred that he had been able to block out all human emotion for so long? Was this to be his parents' final legacy – an inability to feel anything for the suffering of others, his feelings permanently unavailable for comment? It had never occurred to him as being anything unusual, anything out of the ordinary. Life is nasty, brutish and short. Life's a bitch and then you die, he'd always thought. No emotional investment required.

Seeing Felipe on that operating table, no fight left within him, had triggered something in the boy. An overwhelming sense of injustice. Life snatched away before he had a chance to make any choices; good or bad, right or wrong. A whole imagined future of dreams and possibilities rendered obsolete in his final, pitiful breath. With Felipe's death, now the parents were the victims. Oh, the poor things. Undeserving of such a terrible affliction, what more can be done to ease their suffering. Everything upside down. Nothing in its proper order. It was the parents who were *responsible* for the death, the boy reasoned. No matter their age, what kind of *moron* takes a three-week-old baby on such a long journey? This wasn't about simpering sympathy any more. This was about injustice. The righting of something very wrong. The natural order of things.

The boy's mind flashed back. He thought of the countless victims over the years. Of Clare, forever broken. Sally bleeding out in her padded cell, alone in the world. And then there were the insufferables. Colette so bitter and twisted. The Evans so unconflicted. Amy minus the back of her head. Something higher was guiding him towards a destiny. He began to see a way he could channel all his unreleased anger at the injustice of the world. His position gave him unique access to this untapped misery. For those who felt it he could gently guide them in the right direction. For those unable to see it he could offer them clarity. The way things had been so clear in Amy's mind when she picked up Glock number 9 with a round already in the chamber ready to go or for Sally when she played that Jewel CD for the final time. These two had found a release. Now he would help the others to find theirs.

For the Ferreiras he had to act fast. No time to wait for an inquest or hospital review. The boy knew what had to be done soon. They were due to leave the country any day now. Things to organise. A tiny body to repatriate. If they were going to be released from their burden, the boy needed to get to them soon. His mind flashed back to the day of the baby's death, those long hours he spent in their home. He always had a good eye for noticing small details, how insignificant they seemed at the time.

He knew exactly what he was going to do.

Total victim care. The Metropolitan Police Service's commitment to all victims of crime and their families. Every officer involved in the investigation of crime was expected to keep in regular contact with their victims. In the world of serious crime like child abuse or neglect, this included regular home visits. Sometimes this would continue for months or even years after the case had closed. This was his way in.

'Hello?'

The young ex-father barely able to mouth this single word through the latched door of his uncle's Lewisham flat, the tell-tale stench of cigarette smoke emanating through the open door. He hadn't slept much in the past few days, each day and night blurring into one long, unbroken nothingness.

'We spoke on the phone, Mr Ferreira. May I come in?'

The boy needed to be inside quickly, the fewer people who saw him there the better. He had already made sure only the young couple responsible would be home; the older relatives he would spare this time. He needed to make sure this looked right.

'I'm here to help you understand what happens next.'

The advantage with dealing with foreigners is they don't really understand the system, what is normal and what isn't. For all they knew, this was completely normal. The boy needed to use every advantage at his disposal. They were responsible. They had to feel that.

'And your partner, is she here?'

He couldn't risk two visits. This had to be done tonight.

'Yes, she's sleeping in the next room,' Ferreira indicated with his finger through his broken English.

Perfect. Everything in its place. He created some pretence to wander into the kitchen, accidentally of course, quickly opening the valves on all four gas hobs. The tell-tale smell of natural gas, artificially added in case of danger. He was grateful for the fact they had gone for the cheaper gas option; it made things much easier. He didn't have much time now. Ferreira too grief-stricken and over-tired to have noticed.

Any crime scene is meticulously photographed, folders of rather dull room aspects showing exactly where everything was found by the police. These photos could then be produced as exhibits and used in suspect interviews later. It was a well-rehearsed method. Only the surroundings were different this time. And they were most definitely not being tape-recorded.

The boy said nothing. There was a brown coffee table standing in front of a tattered old sofa, covered with old blankets to hide years of wear and tear, no doubt. A packet of Marlboro cigarettes half-empty lay on top of some magazines. Perfect.

Still without speaking, the boy began laying out the photos, one by one. At first just the baby's room. Small yellow ducks on a sky-blue blanket, draped over the side of the Moses basket the baby had been sleeping inside. Tears instantly formed in the young Brazilian man's eyes.

Next the baby's mobile, hanging over the basket. A small red car. A little blue van. All to help baby sleep.

Now Felipe himself on the hospital slab. Lifeless.

Ferreira crumpled into a heap on the floor, barely able to process what lay before him. Re-living those terrible moments over and over. Still no sign of movement from the bedroom next door.

The smell of gas began to fill the room by now. The boy always had an acute sense of smell, not a blessing in an office full of sweaty detectives but useful to him on this occasion. Ferreira still lay on the floor, the tears and anguish seemed to exude every pore in his body. Now we're getting close, thought the boy. This was how it should end. By some twisted moral code, in his mind he was fighting for the shattered dreams and unfulfilled ambitions of Felipe by making his neglectful parents suffer. No chance of redemption. No permission granted to move on.

The gas smell began to envelop every room like an invisible smog. The boy needed to act quickly now or he'd be caught in the ensuing inferno. He quickly gathered the photos, gently prising the image of the dead baby from Ferreira's clammy hands. He took out a cigarette from the opened packet and offered it to his intended victim. Great thing about having an addiction, it never lets you down, thought the boy.

He was too close. He'd been in there too long already. Grief of this magnitude needed to be nurtured, which took time. An abrupt exit would have looked suspicious. Flammable vapours would have secreted into his clothing by now. The recently bereaved mother still lay sleeping in the room next door, oblivious to the carnage about to engulf her.

They'd failed their son. Too stupid to consider the consequences. They had to pay for their stupidity the same price Felipe had so tragically paid.

The boy looked for a light to ignite the flames of Felipe's vengeance. As a non-smoker himself this was something he wouldn't normally carry. Everything had to appear as normal as possible. He panicked as he saw Ferreira slip a hand gingerly into his pocket and produce a small silver Zippo, probably a knock-off. This was it. He couldn't back out now. He made a dash for the door. Luckily in such a small flat this wasn't more than a few steps but his timing had to be perfect. He still had a flight of stairs to run down before he reached the relative sanctity of being outside.

Nothing.

Shit.

He waited, edging slowly away as he did.

BOOM.

Every window from the small flat smashed, sending tiny shards of glass raining down on the car park below. The distraction gave the boy just about enough time to place the crime scene photos back into his unmarked police car and gather some police cordon tape and a high visibility jacket. If he sped away now, it would look suspicious. He had a duty of care to the victims to consider.

The next few minutes were crucial. He had to delay making the 999 call just long enough for the flames and smoke to overcome his two victims upstairs. A typical response time was around twelve minutes. If he stood there looking official in a Hi-Vis busying himself with the familiar blue and white cordon tape, people would assume help was already on the way. There were only so many variables he could control. Eventually, he had to make the call.

'There's been a terrible accident.'

CHAPTER 21

That had been far too close for comfort, David sat in the inspector's office, thinking to himself. Not only had he placed himself directly at the scene of a double murder-suicide, he'd barely got out of there in time himself. Arrogantly assuming he was in control of everything, Ferreira could easily have lit up a cigarette at any time. He was happy with the outcome, but it had been a stupid risk to take. There had to be easier ways for him to bring peace to all the others without endangering himself so much.

'Are you alright, David, you've been through a lot recently? You know that the Met has a confidential counselling service available 24/7 if you need to talk about things with anyone,' the DI said in earnest as he handed over the occupational health card from his drawerful.

Arse-covering. This is what the Met did best. Any death where there has been very recent police contact was bound to attract controversy. All appropriate boxes had to be ticked. If he was suspected of any involvement the conversation would be taking place with a higher rank. If they weren't taking their potential exposure seriously enough it would be with a lower rank. They seemed to have got the level about right.

David had to tread carefully here. He'd done enough to make sure he wasn't implicated in the tragic murder-suicide of the Ferreiras. Mr Ferreira's death almost instant from the blast after – by some amazing good fortune – he'd actually walked into the kitchen as he lit the cigarette. There wasn't much left of him. The kitchen being the epicentre of the blast had taken out the wall leading to the exit for her, so she'd been overcome by smoke inhalation fairly quickly. When the fire rescue team and ambulance crew finally got to her, they did what they could. But she was gone. The family now reunited. Such a tragedy, the local news reported, an entire family wiped out in a matter of days, the young parents unable to live with the loss of their infant.

David had planned it carefully, despite the risk to himself. There was a history of suicide in the family which always played well and there was no CCTV on the communal flat entrance to reveal his visit actually took place. To the rest of the world, David had arrived just moments too late to save them from themselves. Now he needed to play along for a short while, let things run their course. He couldn't have another victim so soon after.

But David felt sure of one thing, despite the risk – he felt no remorse. No anguish. No pain. These people deserved to die, and he had helped to deliver that fate.

'Furthermore, I have seen under the sun that in the place of justice there is wickedness and in the place of righteousness there is wickedness.'
(Ecclesiastes 3:16)

The next few weeks were a strange time for David. He spent most evenings thinking about the image of baby Felipe, permanently etched on to the forefront of his mind. His drinking became more and more frequent, spilling over in to the daytimes and even the mornings on some occasions. Perhaps the lowest point of any man's life is the point at which they find themselves queueing to buy alcohol before licensing hours have officially started. Mothers steering their children away from the strange man with the bottle of brandy in one hand and breakfast in the other. This was acceptable to his colleagues though – after all, he'd been through a lot recently. Nothing to worry about here. This was how police officers were supposed to heal. He'd never felt so embraced and accepted by the rest of the team as he did after killing the Ferreiras.

Kath kept her distance though.

There were questions to answer and enquiries to be made, but eventually the fuss died down and things returned to normal.

Time for the next one.

Colette weighed heavily on his mind. That bitch and her vile, vindictive intentions could not go unpunished. But perhaps not the ultimate price the Ferreiras paid. Something much more suited to her crime.

Colette wasn't finding life as easy as she'd hoped since throwing out Darrell. She had slipped into the meaningless 'booty call' world of so many women on the estate. A man came around when he was needed, which suited both parties.

Because none of them wanted to be around her the rest of the time.

It had become fairly normal for a different man to appear at the door on different nights of the week. The two young children got used to staying in their rooms on those nights. Mummy got very angry if they didn't. They knew when it was one of those times by what Mummy was wearing. Or not wearing. It's amazing the things children pick up.

David hadn't exactly endeared himself to Colette the last time around, so he needed to stay well clear of her this time. But he did have full access to her file, enabling him to set up a fake profile on the dating app Tinder using an old phone he'd fished out of the evidence room. He began sending messages to Errol, recently

117

released from prison for a violent rape charge. Not his first one either. This was a guy who shouldn't be too difficult to bait, thought David.

'oi big boi.'

'lukin for no-stringz.'

'u feelin it?'

The hardest part for David was the fucking moronic way these people communicated, like consonants were an optional extra. But he'd read enough of them in evidence to understand the fine art of moron-speak. No big words. Errol took the bait.

'yeh grrl u lukin a nice ting.'

'wanna beat dat long time.'

A date and time was fixed. The next part was crucial. Errol had to know what he was going to do that evening in words he could understand.

'me like it ruff innit.'

'like PROPER ruff, u get me.'

Errol couldn't believe his luck. He didn't mind prison; he'd been in and out most of his life and knew how to survive. Violence bred into him from an early age to survive the neighbourhood, he could take care of himself. But he missed the pussy on the outside. Creating a Tinder profile was the first thing he did when he got out.

'wot u like?'

Colette didn't give a fuck when she threw her man out and took away his children. Took away his home, his car and everything he worked for his whole life thanks to a family court system hopelessly skewed in women's favour. Embittered fathers dressing up as Batman or Spiderman and scaling the Houses of Parliament hadn't done much to help Darrell. Not content with knowing she'd probably get everything, she made sure of it with some vile allegation, forever tainting his relationship with his son. And she still walked away with two-thirds of everything. Now she was going to pay the price.

'want u2 RAPE me bruv.'

'no safeword, u bust in n just hurt me, for real.'

'wen I scream u keep goin.'

'save this chat on ur fone to cover urself ltr.'

Errol couldn't believe his luck. Colette was about to see hers change. Forever.

'However, each one of you also must love his wife as he loves himself, and the wife must respect her husband.'

(Ephesians 5:33)

Darrell looked after the children at his mum's house for a while after that evening. Mummy wasn't feeling too hot after Errol had raped her repeatedly the second she opened the door to him. He'd given her a beating for good measure, puncturing her lung and rupturing her spleen. It was beautiful. Her screams only added to his excitement. She stopped seeing men for a long time and begged Darrell to come back and protect her. He stayed strong; she was damaged goods. Errol would spend the next twelve years behind bars for the attack. The judge noted, when sentencing, his complete lack of remorse. The fake Tinder profile remained a mystery, the phone and SIM card used both destroyed before the attack even took place. As David knew, it was irrelevant in English law as nobody can consent to extreme violence against themselves.

David tried to imagine a world in which they could.

CHAPTER 22

Dissociative identity disorder – often known as multiple personality disorder – is thought to be a complex psychological condition caused by many factors, including severe trauma during early childhood – usually physical, sexual, or emotional abuse. Most of us have experienced mild dissociation like daydreaming or getting lost in the moment while working on a project. However, dissociative identity disorder is a severe form of dissociation, a mental process which produces a lack of connection in a person's thoughts, memories, feelings, actions, or sense of identity. The dissociative aspect is thought to be a coping mechanism – the person literally dissociates himself from a situation or experience that's too violent, traumatic, or painful to assimilate with his conscious self.

Understanding the development of multiple personalities is difficult, even for highly trained experts. The diagnosis itself remains controversial among mental health professionals, with some experts believing that it is really an 'offshoot' phenomenon of another psychiatric problem, such as borderline personality disorder, or the product of profound difficulties in coping abilities or stresses related to how people form trusting emotional relationships with others.

David had kept himself distant from Colette's little visitation last month and managed to stay completely off the radar. Women of a certain demographic were always making these kinds of allegations when the man didn't do what they wanted, people would say. It was a path well-trodden, and Errol was just another violent man who couldn't keep his dick in his trousers. This is what they don't teach police recruits at training school. Everybody joins with a profound sense of right and wrong, a strong moral code to help the victims and punish the villains. But they don't prepare you for how blurred that line often is. What the court records nine months later as an innocent *victim* often turns out to really be a convicted drug user and former prostitute, or an abuser of her own children through neglect and failing to meet their proper needs. The criminal justice system is something these people use as a means to an end for some perceived need. When you filter out the reams of lies and deceit from a person's background, there are very few *innocent* victims. There are just the consequences of the decisions people make. Hindus call it *karma*. Colette understood this now.

The boy needed to feel close to the next one. He hadn't forgotten seeing how ravaged by depression and misery Clare had become. How she's allowed herself to be a hostage her entire life, never breaking free of the alleged suffering she was forced to endure. If others could deal with it and move on, why couldn't she? She was wasting the gift of life her Catholic god had granted her, a shell of a person, human in name only.

'In their hearts human beings plan their course, but the LORD establishes their steps.'
    (Proverbs 16:9)

She had been given enough chances, enough time to overcome her demons. And she had failed.

'Hello, Clare, I came to see how you're doing.'

The overwhelming stench of body odour, cigarette smoke and alcohol assaulted the boy's senses as he stepped into Clare's dingy council flat on the fifteenth floor. The lift had broken so she hardly went out any more, only to top up her addictions. What had once been white frilly lace curtains now blocked out all natural light, a shade of grey-brown barely distinguishable from the peeling walls. Thick, smoky air seemed to just hang in the room. The boy had worn his less expensive clothes that day, anticipating what he might find.

The last time they had met, Clare had managed to drag her stinking, hulking mass along to the police station. Now seeing her in her natural surroundings she seemed even more pitiful. The product of a welfare system that gives these people no ambition to improve or change their lives, just fattens them up for an eventual early death. Her council flat would be hastily cleared to make way for the next ingrate. The boy was here to accelerate that process.

So often just a box to tick, this welfare visit had a more altruistic aim. To end Clare's suffering. She was already fairly close to the edge. She just needed a little encouragement. The boy had checked her file – three previous suicide attempts.

She wasn't trying hard enough.

He needed to be brutal, land blow after blow on her sense of self-worth. First on the agenda was her case. How nobody believed her and she was not considered credible as a witness. How the fact she had waited forty years and then jumped on the Saville bandwagon made her difficult to take at face value. The boy paused to pour her a drink. A large measure of some brown liquid in a filthy glass left out on what had once been a clean surface. He poured himself one too. She downed hers quickly. He regaled her with stories of successful convictions he had achieved in cases similar to hers, if only she'd spoken out sooner. Now it was too late. All she had done was humiliate herself for nothing.

'But I couldn't tell anybody,' she eventually wailed, tears cascading from her face.

He went on. All the hours he had wasted looking into her case when there were other more deserving victims he should have been helping. The fact she had never married or had children showed nobody else believed her, he said. She had just concocted a little story for attention, like countless other miserable specimens out there ever since victimhood became the *zeitgeist*. He poured her another drink.

'The best thing you can do now is just kill yourself, Clare. You have nothing left to live for.'

Sometimes people just need to be given direction in their lives.

'He will wipe every tear from their eyes. There will be no more death' or mourning or crying or pain, for the old order of things has passed away.'
(Revelations 21:4)

By now they were out on the long, communal balcony outside her flat. Fresh air at last, the boy's gag reflex just about intact. She wailed so uncontrollably loudly the boy worried she might attract attention. But no need to worry. Misery and suffering were *par for the course* around these parts. Part of the inner-city deprived landscape. She clutched the cheap whiskey bottle in her hand the way a child holds a comfort blanket, sucking on the opening to ease her anxiety.

He had to act quickly. He couldn't wait around all day for her to make the decision for herself; he needed to be certain. Judging by her size and probable weight, she needed to be right on the edge for this to work. If she fell to the balcony floor, he'd never get her up again and would have some awkward explaining to do. At least he had the advantage of her being so intoxicated any account she might give would be completely unreliable. *Plus ca change.* But he was determined that wouldn't be necessary. He seized his moment. Clare had turned facing outwards, sobbing hysterically, both hands on the rail. If he could get the required lift, she'd have no chance to recover her balance in time.

He slowly adjusted his position backwards towards the door a few feet. He needed a very fast up-and-over action and he only had one chance to get it right. All those dead-lifts in the gym were about to pay off, he hoped. He lunged forwards, burying his head between her disgusting, fat sweaty thighs from behind and lifted with all the strength he could muster. She weighed a fucking tonne, he thought to himself, though this came as no surprise. If his momentum hadn't been sufficient, her weight on top of him would surely have permanently damaged his spinal column. Not to mention the stink of her matted pubic mass wedged into his neck like a sweaty pillow through the standard-issue leggings fat people insist on wearing in all weathers.

Then there was no weight at all, as she fell fifteen floors.

Fifteen chances to think about all the years she might have lived beyond that moment.

Fifteen seconds to consider the choices she had made leading up to this point.

And then nothing.

A dark burgundy pool emanated from the remnants of her collapsed skull, quickly filling the cracks between the concrete paving slabs beneath. Some children playing nearby screamed, and a small crowd began to appear out of every nook and cranny of the estate. Another jumper. Must be near the end of the month.

Slowly, all eyes turned upwards to his position, high above the blood and bone *melee* below. The next part was crucial. As her mass came quickly downwards, she had pushed the boy's chest and shoulders onto the railings as she slid forward into the abyss. He stayed in this position as it mimicked the position you might expect to see a concerned neighbour peer over the edge into the horror below. Everything planned. Everything in its place. Even concern for the dead was something he had to fabricate.

He would tell the officers who arrived on scene that he tried to stop her. He was here explaining to her the realities of her weak case, and he never would have intended her to react this way.

By jumping to her death below.

CHAPTER 23

Since learning of the abuse suffered by her two young children at the hands of the male nanny she hired, Mrs Anel Evans had maintained a sense of stunned indifference at which the upper-classes are so capable. A new nanny hastily acquired, the children sent away on endless re-education activities to erase any lingering memory of Roberto. As if nothing ever happened.

The boy could not allow this.

Another mother who failed her children and then compounded her mistake by failing to change her ways. *She* should be looking after her *own* children, the boy thought. When a down-at-heel family on a council estate chose to leave their children with friends and relatives for a few hours, they are judged negatively. Yet when the McCanns leave their three children completely unsupervised on holiday in Portugal – one of them never to be seen again – they are paraded as middle-class victims of a vile kidnapping. So, when a family like the Evans' pay somebody to more or less raise the children for them, this is deemed socially acceptable. The world turned upside down.

He watched the Evans' family routine from a distance. He had time on his hands since his suspension on full pay. Those morons at professional standards wouldn't find anything they could pin on him, and he'd be back at work in no time, the boy knew. People commit suicide all the time. Weakness leaving the gene pool, nature's own way of thinning the herd. He was merely expediting the process. This one wouldn't be so easy as Clare or the Ferreiras, who had vulnerabilities he could exploit. Pampered indifference wasn't a character asset he could use. He had to make Anel care, make her see where her priorities should really be.

'Whoever brings ruin on their family will inherit only wind, and the fool will be servant to the wise.' (Proverbs 11:29)

Everybody out into the ridiculously over-sized family SUV – standard issue in these parts – then off on the school run. Usually back to the house around nine a.m. for some leisurely indifference. Then most days out again around eleven a.m. for the usual opportunities to be seen in the right places, the norm for those like her with no need to worry about such trivialities as money or having meaningful purpose. Droves of haughty women arriving at hair salons and day spas like an occupying force in a fleet of German-made SUVs, marching on to have loud lunches and café au lait in the most conspicuous locations. Then off to collect the kids from school around three p.m. and back home to reflect on such a tiring day as the children are immediately handed off to the new nanny. The whole charade made the boy feel sick.

The morning after returning from the school run was his opportunity. He didn't want to have to scar the children too badly this time. Unlike Colette's two. They'd seen too much. The boy hadn't intended this but he hadn't anticipated just how loud and for how long a woman with a prolapsed rectum can scream. Errol had been the perfect animal. He just kept going and going, ripping and tearing as she tried vainly to fight him off. All part of the act, Errol assumed. He'd even had the brazen confidence to just sit by her bleeding, weeping body when he'd finally had his fill, only becoming vaguely concerned that perhaps he had misjudged the situation as she dialled 999 and just screamed into the receiver. Time to leave, Errol correctly realised, noticing the two children sat trembling with fear as he left.

This time would be different, the boy said to himself. Quick and clean. But he had to act fast. He'd parked a distance away and lay in wait behind the large planter that the Evans had installed, mostly because it was bigger than the large planter the house next door had installed the previous summer. As she returned and drove into the remotely-opened garage, he slipped in behind her, his Drager X-plore 3300 half-face respiratory mask already in place. The next part was all about timing. He slid into the back seat as she applied the handbrake and the garage door closed automatically behind them. He quickly bound her hands behind her – she was too shocked and dignified to scream, just helplessly gasping in mouthfuls of the toxic exhaust fumes slowly filling the garage. With Anel secure in position in the driver's seat, the boy lowered all four windows of the SUV. It was important that the ligatures around her wrists were not bound too tightly, as they could show tell-tale marks. This had to appear natural. Panic caused her to gasp in bigger mouthfuls of unhealthy air, until she stopped moving.

And ye shall tread down the wicked; for they shall be ashes under the soles of your feet.
(Malachi 4:3)

CHAPTER 24

The administrative leave continued, professional standards going into hyperdrive over the continued death of those recently in contact with David. Colette's little night-time visitation by Errol hadn't been connected to him in any way yet, but four apparent suicides within a few months of each other meant he appeared on the radar of people increasingly higher up the food chain. The kinds of people you might see doing press conferences with lots of crowns and wreaths on their shoulder.

David's recollection of events was patchy at best, his connection to these events increasingly vague. He had been careful. No phones that could be tracked to give away his historic locations. He knew all about Locard's principle of exchange, that the perpetrator of a crime will always leave something behind at the scene. The clothes he had worn that day had been burned afterwards. Besides, he had divine help; he need not worry about the judgment of his fellow man.

He sat staring over the precipice at Beachy Head, his favourite spot. He enjoyed the peace and serenity of knowing he was inches from death at any time, only his strength and will keeping him with the living. Barely thirty minutes before he'd arrived there had been significant rock fall as part of the cliff just fell into the sea.

The advantage of being suspended was it kept his caseload down, so his victims were few in number. Just a few more to go now.

One from the past.

One from the present.

And one for the future.

Lloyd had never amounted to much, as is so often the case in children showing deviant proclivities at a young age. When children commit grotesque offences, society often struggles to comprehend its progeny. No case was this more apparent than the shocking murder of two-year-old Jamie Bulger in 1993 by Robert Thompson and Jon Venables. Parents who had separated; both boys had difficulties with attendance, learning and behaviour at school. They bunked off, they shoplifted, they were violent; all these pieces in a pattern that made up a pair of empty, broken young lives. Before their trial in November 1993, the press ferreted around the doorways and back alleys of Walton village, Liverpool, looking for anything that might determine that these two ten-year-olds were indeed evil or the product of evil. Neighbours told of pigeons having their heads shot off with an airgun, of rabbits being tied to railway lines, of dawn roller booting sessions. There were tales of charity collection boxes being stolen and of children being assaulted in the classroom.

Exaggeration and gossip aside, a picture of neglect slowly emerged, a picture that focused on the pair's 'bad parents'. Ann Thompson was portrayed as an incompetent alcoholic, while Susan Venables was painted as a loose woman whose neighbours 'noted a procession of men friends for Mrs Venables'. A narrative emerged of two childhoods influenced not merely by the flaws of parents or the absence of a father, but by the environment in which these boys lived, a world of social and economic deprivation, of trashy television and cultural poverty, inadequate social services, failed schooling and general confusion.

It was a place that left a moral vacuum for two children who would go on to kill and leave the unanswered question: why did they do it? Thompson was a member of what can only be described as a terribly dysfunctional family. The fifth of seven children, he proved as difficult to his mother as the rest of her brood. Ann Thompson had been deserted by her husband five years before the killing of Jamie Bulger, and in the week after he left, the family home burned down in an accidental fire. Left on her own, Thompson sought consolation in drink and was often to be found in the bar rather than looking after the children in her chaotic home, where bedlam ensued. The boys, it was later reported, grew up 'afraid of each other'. They bit, hammered, battered and tortured each other.

In summary – children are a product of their environment.

Venables later developed his interests beyond slaughtering toddlers towards the sexual exploitation of them, his moral compass forever askew. Why people do the things they do will always be the subject of academic and social debate.

The boy wasn't interested in any of that. He never even saw what had happened to him as being particularly harmful. But he had seen enough adult abuse of children to know it was wrong.

'Then shall ye return, and discern between the righteous and the wicked, between him that serveth God and him that serveth him not.'
(Malachi 3:18)

These people were mercifully predictable, Lloyd having grown up in an environment not dissimilar to Thompson and Venables. Lack of ambition combined with lack of aspiration kept him firmly entrenched in the mire of social deprivation he had grown up in. Finding him did not prove difficult, barely two streets from the council house he grew up in. He lived alone, an absent father to several children scattered around the estate, replete in *de rigueur* tracksuit bottoms and trainers. Not that he did any sporting activity that might require stamina or determination, the boy noted in his preparations.

The beating he delivered would be his crowning moment of pure, unadulterated rage. Lloyd lay helplessly on the hallway floor as blow after blow rained down on him from the boy's Slugger baseball bat, the dark crimson seeping into the tired old carpet. There were bound to have been other victims. Other children forced to partake in his sordid proclivities. Each blow to the head was a blow in return for each of his victims over the years. The boy had no intention to kill Lloyd that day. Lloyd would discover his fate in due course.

'Do you know who I am?'

'No, I've never seen you before, please stop. I'll give you money, whatever you want,' begged Lloyd, blood oozing from various cuts around his head and his left eye half-closed from swelling.

'You will give me something. But first you need to understand who I am. Look again.'

Lloyd wasn't lying; he didn't have a clue. The boy looked very different standing before him that day from the scrawny nine-year-old boy he was the last time they met. There had been others over the years.

'I don't know who you are. I'm sorry for whatever I did.'

He dragged Lloyd onto a nearby chair. The boy reminded him of that visit to the waterworks all those years ago. Lloyd's face sank. He didn't remember but

136

knew it was something he had done to others. Trying desperately to think of some way to appease his attacker, Lloyd panicked and said the last thing the boy needed to hear:

'I didn't hurt you, did I?'

He needed Lloyd awake and conscious for what followed. No abused person ever needs to hear their abuser try to justify or excuse their actions. It only makes things worse. Lloyd fell to the floor from the force of the blow that followed.

The boy was using his elbow now; the bat would cause severe concussion and most likely death if he had carried on using it. The mistake many amateurs make when they try to hurt somebody is they punch like they've seen people do in movies. Big hay-makers with loose fists crashing into the skull, the hardest part of the human body. The boy had seen plenty broken wrists and shattered pinkie-fingers over the years to know this. He knew it was far more effective to use the hardened tools your body has given you – knees and elbows. These bones don't break so easily.

The boy dragged Lloyd onto a chair for the next part of the punishment. Lloyd was bleeding heavily now and beginning to lose consciousness. The boy produced a list of websites from the so-called *dark web*, a sordid underworld of narcotics and child pornography on sale for the customer who knew how to find it. With the

Slugger held to his right cheek, Lloyd was instructed to enter specific search terms on his *own* computer.

'rim job, child'

'anal fisting eight-year-old boy'

'torn vagina, five-year-old girl'

And so it went. Lloyd forced to watch each degrading, humiliating act in full, having paid for the privilege to do so using his own credit card. His only alternative was to die a slow, painful death, the boy explained to him.

The abuser's mindset is completely self-centred, thinking only of the pleasure they receive from a situation and nothing of the misery and humiliation they inflict, even just passively by paying others to carry out the acts for their titillation. Watching these children suffer as they were forced to commit unspeakable acts, Lloyd wanted it to stop. Sure, over the years he'd had a few kids wank him off and on one occasion got a blowjob from a twelve-year-old girl, but nothing on the scale of depravity he was being forced to watch now. He wasn't a monster. Lloyd prayed it would soon be over.

Eventually enough. The damage was done, wheels set in motion. The boy and Slugger melted away into the night. Lloyd spent the next few weeks passing blood in his stool and urine, as internal wounds slowly healed. He decided not to go to the police, realising they would soon be coming anyway. Every internet user has a unique *internet protocol (IP)* address; the boy knew *any* of the forbidden sites he had forced Lloyd to access would flag up immediately and his arrest would duly follow. These were absolute offences. The charge sheet would simply read *on day/date/time/place you downloaded illegal content*. There was no defence, no justification. When eventually released from prison he would forever be on the sex offenders register, a minor inconvenience. What worried him more was the promise of further vengeance the boy had made him.

'It is mine to avenge; I will repay. In due time their foot will slip; their day of disaster is near and their doom rushes upon them.'
(Deuteronomy 32:35)

CHAPTER 25

He was getting close now. The past had been dealt with, for now. Lloyd would spend the rest of his days looking over his shoulder, sleeping with one eye open. Professional standards had fished around enough to allow David back to work. The only connection the victims had was circumstantial in the sense that they had been David's recent cases. But so had hundreds of others in the past and what the Met needed more than anything was boots on the ground, foot soldiers to investigate the six-fold increase in reported cases of child abuse since the publicity surrounding the Saville enquiry. David was fully reinstated without prejudice. Now he had an internal matter of his own to deal with.

Gary was a violent prick who beat his wife repeatedly over their two-year marriage. An architect by trade, his use of steroids and endless hours in the gym after work gave him a very unpredictable temperament his Cuban wife Marisa came to know only too well. The black eyes, the broken noses, the bruised arms and lower back. Many trips to hospital, 'I fell' she would always say, too afraid of the consequences of reporting anything to the police. Like so many women, trapped in a loveless violent marriage because she hadn't the strength to escape. David didn't have much sympathy with people like this.

If you choose to sleep in the lion's den, don't be surprised if he bites you once in a while.

Eventually Marisa found the strength to leave Gary, taking their two-year-old daughter with her back to her native Cuba. Gary was incandescent with rage. The law surrounding parental abduction by removing your own child from one country to another is complex, to say the least. If the child concerned is a dual national, there is very little anyone can do to bring the child back, beyond making a polite request through diplomatic channels. This would be the case with any country but even more so with a country like Cuba which hasn't always enjoyed entirely harmonious relations with the West and where trust between the two is often a scarce commodity. None of this helped Gary's rage at losing his daughter.

Although Marisa had never found the courage to report the matter herself, some friends and close neighbours had tried to help. Without a victim willing to substantiate, the police could do very little in the past. Just another 'domestic disturbance' the report would say. The existence of so many third-party reports did not go in Gary's favour, however, when he came to report his daughter's abduction by the mother.

'Good on her, he's a complete wanker,' Kath shared with the office.

'Got what he deserved,' another jumped on the bandwagon.

David wasn't going to publicly agree with Kath on anything, even if deep down he felt a fair outcome had been achieved. He knew the damage growing up in a violent home could cause and was happy for the daughter who would be spared this indignity.

David understood what made violent men tick, having seen so many. He had been allocated quite a few cases like this over the years in recognition of this fact, his ability to establish *rapport* with violent lunatics had not gone unnoticed. With the right amount of stage-management, they could be useful in certain situations.

'Kath, do you think you could help me out on this case?'

David's question in front of the whole office caught her completely off guard. They had barely acknowledged each other's existence for months. But when a colleague asks for help, even someone you don't particularly like, it would reflect badly on her if she refused. To serve without fear or favour, they had all signed up for after all.

'No problem.' Kath seethed through gritted teeth.

Angry men who beat their wives usually don't respond well to haughty women interfering and telling them what they think. David just needed to set the scene. He agreed with Kath to visit Gary alone in the first instance to establish *rapport*, then they would go back together later for a full statement. David had had plenty of people accuse him over the years of being blunt, too direct or even rude sometimes – ninety percent of the time this came from weak people who couldn't handle the truth. He didn't expect to have any problems with Gary.

'Hello, Gary, we spoke on the phone. Just need to run through some details with you.'

'No worries, come in.'

Gary had dressed for the occasion. Bare-chested and shorts only. It was his home they were in after all; why should he make an effort? The message he was sending to David was clear.

Do not fuck with me.

David explained the legal position to Gary and ran through the various potential outcomes, the main one being it was unlikely they could bring his daughter back to the UK. They could seek to extradite his wife and prosecute her for child abduction, but this would take a long time. Gary was belligerent, to say the least.

'I don't fucking care. I want that fucking cunt to pay for what she has done to me.'

Now you're the victim, David thought to himself. These morons are full of sympathy for themselves when things don't go their way, but have no regard for the law or for other people any other time. Everybody wants to be a victim these days.

'Absolutely, we will do everything we can, sir.'

David then explained what might slow the process down a little.

'You see, Gary, I have to work within a team of professionals who all want to do the best they can for the children first and foremost. You understand this?'

Gary nodded slowly, his fists clenching.

'Some of my colleagues think you shouldn't have your daughter back because of your violent past.'

He let this sink in, watching Gary's body language very carefully. You learn to spot the early warning signs when someone is about to attack you.

'There's one person I work with in particular,' David continued, 'who is kind of like my supervisor. She doesn't think we should support your case due to the history of domestic violence.'

'I've never been charged or convicted with anything,' Gary fired back at David, 'and you can't refuse to help me just because of some bullshit allegations.'

He was right, of course.

'She's going to come along next time so you can meet her.'

The stage was set. David had been careful not to make any promises, but he'd been able to gauge Gary's temperament. With his usual punch-bag now out of the country, he was a tinderbox waiting to explode.

David relayed the conversation back to Kath later at the office, with a little gilding of the lily here and there for maximum effect. Kath couldn't help herself, her menopausal crusade for women's rights brimming out of every world-weary orifice, outraged that any man would feel victimised by these circumstances.

'I'll set him straight,' Kath pledged with pride.

We'll fucking see about that, David thought to himself.

A few days later, David and Kath were sitting in Gary's living room. He'd taken the trouble to wear a shirt this time, David noticed. What this would portend he did not yet know. From the outset the atmosphere was tense. Gary and Kath both sized each other up, seething inside with judgement and resentment. The years had not been kind to Kath – greasy, bedraggled grey hair, her body ravaged by years of poor diet and minimal exercise. Over a thirty-year career she had seen more misery and anguish at work than most and her face showed every nuance of this. She was a fucking mess.

'What you need to understand, Gary, is that you can't spend years beating your wife up and then act surprised when she leaves you.'

Kath couldn't help herself.

'Frankly, from what I've read about you, your wife has done the safest possible thing for herself and for your child by taking her away from…'

She didn't even get a chance to finish the sentence. Gary had managed to contain his rage for about thirty seconds before laying her out with a savage right hook across the table.

Kath lay in a bloody, crumpled heap on the floor, her jaw broken, groaning in pain. The arrogance of having gone so many years without being hit proving her downfall. Men are better at reading these situations, knowing when to shut up. Kath understood this now, as she spat out two of her molars onto Gary's polished floor.

Gary turned towards David, expecting to be restrained. His face twisted in rage.

David calmly turned to Kath, leaned down towards her and whispered, 'When you are suffering, remember *I* have betrayed you.'

He slowly stood and walked outside, leaving Kath to face the consequences of her actions.

'And the God of all grace, who called you to his eternal glory in Christ, after you have suffered a little while, will himself restore you and make you strong, firm and steadfast.'
(Peter 5:10)

David took the unmarked police car and drove away. He knew Kath never even bothered carrying handcuffs or a baton any more; she felt such things were beneath someone of her stature. She could find her own way out of this situation or die trying, David thought to himself.

It didn't matter. David didn't need the job any more to complete his mission. He knew what the likely consequences would be for him, depending on the severity of Kath's injuries.

Suspension.

Gross Misconduct for Neglect of Duty.

Dismissal.

CHAPTER 26

Kath's injuries were life-changing, though sadly for David not life-threatening. She would spend the next month eating her meals through a straw from a food blender, unable to chew or move her fractured jaw. She was hospitalised for two months due to multiple facial fractures and a swelling on the brain. She had a punctured lung and shattered collar-bone, caused by Gary repeatedly stamping on her weak, defenceless body as she lay in the foetal position begging for her life. Gary would spend the next twelve years behind bars for GBH with intent. Marisa was safe from his reach at last.

Most people raised in a loving and caring environment, where the needs of the child are put first, never truly understand how the absence of this nurturing affects a child's social development. When raised in a climate of constant tension and fear, that child's ability to interact normally and recognise conventional social cues is severely limited. And the further away from that childhood experience the individual grows, often the more focused these issues become in their mind. You may coast through life generally fitting in and getting along with most people you meet, the occasional personality clash here and there. For a child raised with violence forever an imminent prospect, their ability to rise above even trivial annoyances or turn the other cheek weighs heavily on their mind in some perverted zero-sum idea of strength in the face of adversity. To give ground, to concede any point, would betray weakness. And any display of weakness would render you at the mercy of a predator. So better to always project strength through hostility and aggression, the way a rhino's horn serves as a permanent deterrent to his predators. No matter how hard it might try, the rhino cannot simply remove his horn one day. It is part of who he is.

That person may seem normal to the outside world. They may function at a high level, play sports and have a favourite novel just like you. But inside they are empty. Unable to properly love or show warmth and affection, because that crucial part of their upbringing was absent. They grow away from extended family, their existence a permanent reminder to others of something not quite as it should be. They become awkward to be around, their pain forever etched across their face. Most people don't want to be around that while they pull a Christmas cracker or blow out the candles on their birthday cake. Even a smile they can disguise as a grimace. All because deep down their sense of self-worth is so low they don't even believe they are worthy of real love and affection.

Other people are merely transitory – they simply do not matter.

There had been further rock fall earlier that day at Beachy Head, heading westwards towards Birling Gap and the Seven Sisters. The shingle beach below had been closed, some rocks narrowly missing sunbathers' heads by inches. The boy walked along the cliff top, comfortable knowing precisely where the danger lay to his left as he walked towards the small lighthouse on top of the hill. He looked over his shoulder to see his favourite view in the whole world, the calm summer sea gently lapping against the white cliffs, their sheer size and grace matched only by the beauty and tranquillity of the scene set before him.

It had not been difficult to bring his father here. Years in the emotional wilderness had done nothing to dampen his sense of moral superiority. The boy was always too sensitive, he would say. The boy had grown strong, benefitting from the iron hand of his upbringing. Everybody suffers sometime, he insisted.

Something else people not raised in such a lion's den of fear fail to fully appreciate is the disjointed, unpredictable way inner rage manifests itself. Not necessarily against the person it should really be directed towards, any given situation can release years of suppressed anger and despair.

'He was despised and rejected by mankind, a man of suffering, and familiar with pain.'
(Isaiah 53:3)

There was no wave of acknowledgment or recognition from either father or son. Each knew the other's silhouette well by now, the way a rabbit recognises a fox through the long grass. The coastguard helicopter hovered in the distance, inspecting the cliff edge for any signs of further erosion, completely invisible to the two men standing atop the hill, their attention only on each other. They spoke in short, staccato sentences, each one unwilling to fully engage the other for fear of what might spill forth.

'So you like it here?'

His father's unmistakeable sneer. They could be sitting atop the clouds in heaven admiring the Sistine Chapel and his father would find fault somewhere. Nothing would ever change that.

'It's peaceful here,' the boy replied.

There are three instinctive reactions humans have when confronted by a threat: fight, flight or freeze. People always forget about the third option and usually just do one of the first two. Sometimes in the void of inner feeling, doing nothing seems the most apt response.

The boy need not worry about the everyday stress of work any more. His search amongst the hopeless for redemption was over now. Roberto, Lloyd and Gary in prison. Clare, Anel and the Ferreiras at rest. Kath and

Colette forever broken, given time to re-evaluate their choices. The boy had served justice to those in his path.

He felt nothing.

There is a cycle to misery. One child raised a certain way begets another who begets another and so it goes. Every once in a while, one of them manages to wriggle free from beneath the weight that crushes them. But most of them don't.

The boy crept closer to the cliff edge, as he realised he had nothing more to say to his father.

'When you pass through the waters, I will be with you; and when you pass through the rivers, they will not sweep over you. When you walk through the fire, you will not be burned; the flames will not set you ablaze.'

(Isaiah 43:2)